one minus one

episodes and images

by James Macmillan

_____

as related to

Jeremy Witt

inner orbit books

a wander, 1998

To You

black punch, 2000, 2014

"I don't know what you're going to do so I have to be ready."

—overheard conversation

"There is but one way to brave the sorrows: headlong."

—unknown

"I think, perhaps, the way for me to not be afraid of you is for me to make you afraid of me."

—Rep. John Milliken
(on the eve of his conviction)

Grandaddy, 1997

Intro:

So, you want me to write this thing. So I am.

Near, and far, 1997

episodes

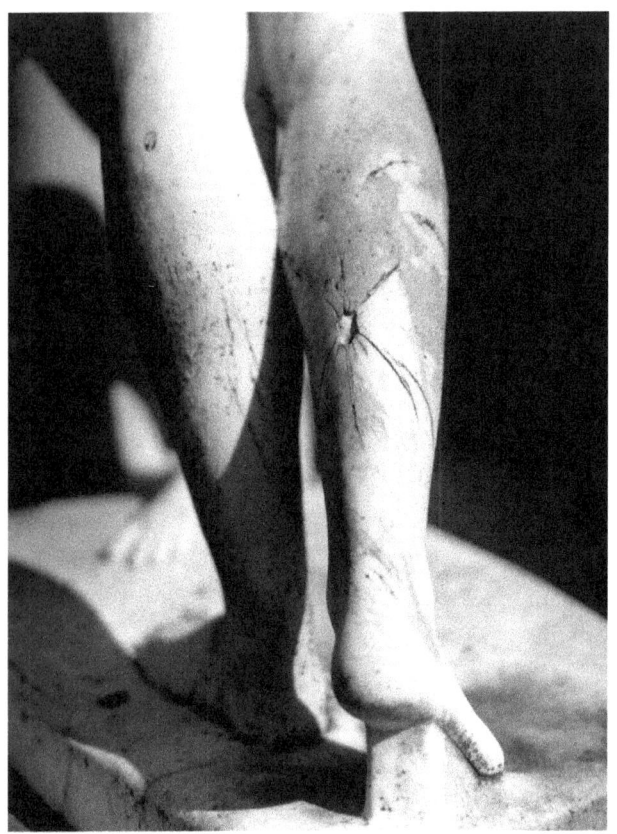

Poise, 2003

Part One

up (and running)

Arizona, 2003

The Sun Devil

The first time it happened I don't think I even noticed. My mind was on other things.

The second time it happened I was more aware, more settled. And well, shit, I heard the shotgun. The blast.

My father died in a drunk driving accident. It was a tragedy really. He had just gotten his bonus check and was bringing it home to my mother and me for Thanksgiving. Of course though, it was raining so driving wasn't good. And there was this big truck, the bright lights, the grass, the guard rail, the trees, the windshield. The world is upside down. Lights out.

At least that's the way my ma described it to me. I wasn't there. I was asleep. Well, sort of. She was pacing. Her noisy back and forth clomping was louder than the pounding rain on the tin roof of our house.

See, I used to live in Virginia. You know, before my father died. Before I came out here.

Tempe Arizona. Dry. Flat. Just like you'd imagine. A desert. No trees. Though there are cactuses. Lots of them. They're cheap substitutes for the big oaks and maples—shit—even the pines—of Virginia.

So I'm not in school right now. It's summer—not that it's any different from winter. And I'm spending a lot of time here—my aunt and uncle's place. It's a trailer. A three room trailer outside of Tempe. I sleep on the couch. I don't like it. But, I had no other choice.

I've been here for two years. I kept thinking it would get better. It hasn't. Except I do laugh every now and then. At my uncle.

He has a lot of time on his hands, shit, I mean hand. See, he doesn't have a right hand. The way he says it, a machine at work tried to eat him. The way they say it is an early pension, small stipend, and keep quiet.

He's a little nuts.

Like this morning. I wake up and his big grizzly face is two inches from my eyeballs. Jesus, I jumped. His ugly, fat, bulbous nose was right there.

I mean, damn! Are you going to kiss me?!

Why would I do that? A giggle, some teeth.

Shit, I don't know Don. That's one good thing. He lets me call him Don. He likes it. I think he feels tougher when people call him Don.

Naw, I ain't gonna kiss ya. I'm just looking at ya. Was ya dreamin'?

I don't know, DON.

Yer eyes was twitchin' all around. Like ya was dreamin'. I think ya was. He turned his back, scratching his head with his hand. I could see the seam of his underwear above his belt.

What? He whipped around.

For a moment we just stared at each other. Then he came forward. This man had never been a father and had no intention of ever even trying. But, if you played him right, he was good for a laugh. Shit, maybe I am dreaming. Nightmare maybe.

His grizzly, half-patchy beard was brushing my face again.

He wouldn't back off. He knew I was thinking something. Something he wouldn't like. I just stared. Don could be scary too, though he didn't mean to be. Randomness is scary, you know, like a dog with that look in its eye. You just know something isn't right. Well, it was that way with Don, a lot I guess.

I gotta go pick some berries. I might need some help. Bad breath. Like a mildewy can. Old soup. Rotten.

He held out his stump for sympathy as he backed away a little. But shit I'll tell you his eyes were laser diamonds. Right at me. Shit, right through me.

Don, why don't you let me wake up for a second.

He dimmed and finally noticed how close he was.

Oh, yeah, OK.

He backed up slowly, unconsciously, rubbing the stump. He always did that when he was uncomfortable.

I felt better when he flopped down in his squeaky vinyl recliner. It was five feet from me, but in that trailer he might as well have been sitting right on my chest. His eyes were still on me as I swung my bare feet to the floor. I rubbed the sleep away and coughed.

Sorry I woke ya. Maybe I'm excited. I don't know. Berries. His eyes glinted again.

Where's Auntie?

She's gone to the store. Supplies.

Supplies for my aunt were tequila and some other stuff—chips, frozen pizza—but mainly tequila. I liked her though. Tequila puts the edge on a lot of people—sharpens the teeth—the serrated edge—but it dulled that natural edge in her right on down. Shit, with my uncle she needed it I guess. And for herself. Her dad abused her, sexually. You know, not so bad.

That's what my ma said. She was there. She was the older one. She wouldn't let grandaddy do that to her. But, you know, she couldn't really stop him from doing it to Auntie. It was survival for her. At least that's what she said when she told me. I think that was before dad died. She probably still feels guilty.

So there's Don staring at me—asking me with his crisp diamond eyes—to help him pick peyote caps—to get the stuff with him. Usually I said no. But today—that day—I figured why not. He'd get them anyway. I might as well help.

In the distance—toward Tempe—a siren whined. Probably a fire truck. It's dry here you know.

How long ago did she leave?

I don't know. An hour. Maybe. She'll be back soon.

Yeah, it's OK. Let's just go. He was getting twitchy. There's not much you can do when my uncle Don gets twitchy.

I stood up. He giggled while twitching. I looked down and noticed my descending erection under my boxer shorts.

Musta been a good 'un. He unconsciously licked his lips. Had he two hands he might have tried something. I was exposed. Nothing to do.

You mean the dream.

Yeah. More giggling.

Don, I'm seventeen. Give me a break.

Yeah, yeah, I know.

I turned and squatted, pulling my shorts from under the couch. My hand brushed the cold metal of his shotgun under there—where it had been since the last time he freaked out. Not much of a dresser—the underneath of a couch—but shit, what was I going to do?

I turned around. You're jealous.

That shut him up. A strike deep at his shriveled manhood.

He jumped up and moved a little too quickly to the kitchen. Hurry up.

I stared at his wide receding back.

He's essentially a good guy. Maybe I was unfair. He only tried something a couple of times before. I don't think he really cares.

—

So we're walking back from picking berries—the caps. He's walking too fast, his mind elsewhere. The brown lunch bag he brought along is heavy at his side. It's full. His stump is swinging happily.

You know how some people find the desert beautiful? I think it's almost beautiful. Sure, yeah, the sun is half way up in the bright blue sky and the colors are rich and full and the expanse is endless—a few mesas and plateaus here and there. And cactuses. But to me it's just flat. Sometimes flat is good. Most of the time it's boring. I'm a visual person. I like things in my line of view—angles, trees, verticals. Horizontal is dull.

So again I'm watching Don's back. His shoulders swayed slightly. In ten years he'll have a hump. But now his vitality was still a reality, not a former glory.

You just going to eat them or what?

I knew something was bad. Something was coming—or growing.

He didn't break stride and in one motion wedged the lunch bag between his right arm and his side. Quickly he peeled the lips apart and hungrily dug into our catch, inside. I mean, Jesus, he was eating them like popcorn at a movie. Gobble gobble. Pieces were dropping out of the corners of his mouth falling to the ground in front of me.

Then I saw our trailer. It was on a little rise. All alone. Auntie's rusty truck was beside it. The crazy house was coming closer with each step. The place where I lived.

—

By the time the old door swung open and my Auntie emerged Don had finished half of the bag. He saw her and tucked it between his elbow and ribs and rolled the top tight.

She didn't look at him as she stopped on the first step. She looked passed him. At me. Her fat cheeks were rosy in the morning light. Her eyes were lean. No tequila yet. Her hands were locked tightly on naturally padded hips. I couldn't help but notice she wasn't wearing a bra and the edges of her saggy breasts peeked from behind the thin straps of her worn house dress.

Under a tattered mess of steely, grey hair her eyes drove right into me—I could feel it in my chest. I knew in that moment that she couldn't wait for me to move on—to move out. Shit. The woman had hope for me. That was what was in her eyes. It was sad, but it was hope still the same. Then BOOM! Don stomped past her into the trailer without a word. She stood firm—still staring at me—but now she was mad.

Why do you help him? Her sad eyes tore right into me.

Why do you encourage him?

Her way of speaking was so much better than his. She could be angry and kind at the same time.

I was at the bottom of the steps, looking up at her. The sun over the trailer gave her this insane halo. I'd lost her eyes.

I don't know.

A shiver ran through her with my words. I could see it. But I knew it wasn't my fault. It was her fault. She believed in me. That was her problem.

How was the store?

It was wrong. I knew. But for once she played along even though she was deflated.

The same. The usual. Nothing new.

He woke me up.

She turned to the side to let me pass into the trailer.

They say it's the little things that mean a lot.

—

Don plucked the tea bag out of his old cup and fixed his glazed eyes on me. I was trying to read and could feel it.

With the index finger of his only hand he nudged his breast. Don's shape I realized was not that different from my Auntie's.

This is what happens, you know.

I looked up. Now he was pinching it, the corner of his mouth tight with pain.

I know it's not fair. I know we all die, blah, blah, blah, BLAH! He squeaked up on his butt in his chair, his eyes focused just past me. That's another thing about Don. He gets lucid when he eats the caps.

I also know that the concept of human dignity is an invention of men like car tires or a building.

Let the games begin.

What about love, Don? I surprised myself with a firm tenor.

Oh Jesus!

He flopped back and I heard Auntie slam a pot in the

kitchen. No secrets in a three room trailer in the desert.

Love! God damn it! Oh I mean it you little seventeen year old fuck! What do you know?!

Only what you tell me Don.

Aha! Bright eyes. Color in the cheeks.

Love holds the keys to truth. Love is a way into the universe. Good God! We stand so separated, walled out by walls that we build. Jesus! He looked up at the low ceiling. Did he really see Jesus?

But Don, we need walls. Structure. Don't you think? I had no idea what I was saying. As long as I kept him talking, his fury would eventually pass. This I did know.

I think a lot. I think for everybody because somebody's got to do it. You little pissant kid. What do you do? He jumped up wildly rubbing his stump.

Again Auntie slammed a pot.

He heard it.

What do you know? You droopy old lady. You're here with me. What good is that? He turned back to me.

With this motherless, fatherless refugee of the world. Good God, don't you see? You choose. Life is whatever you want it to be. He always said this.

I think he knew he was insane—on the way out—and I think he liked it.

For God sakes! If you want love—if you want to see it—then good—whoopee! Go buy some at the store! Wildly rubbing the stump, eyes searching for the brown lunch bag. Beginning to drool.

But you know what? Love matters—it's the one thing that matters—it's the one thing that's real. Everything else is an invention.

Somehow I knew he was right.

Why Don? It was her. Good god, we needed music. They were starting to dance.

Why? That is a stupid question. If you were paralyzed, lying in the street near death with nothing to protect you or to conceal you, you would know love—you would feel it—see it—smell it! God! So many people! Shit! Everybody spends their whole lives trying to get back to love. Real, unencumbered, potent love!

His eyes were searching more intently.

She knew it. Her eyes were fire as she sashayed around the room stopping in front of his recliner. He was coming near me on the couch. He was twitching bad. Then he found the bag beside the couch, snatched it up, and gobbled a handful of caps. I had no idea what would happen.

But Don, I love you.

I actually heard his teeth grind. He turned, but couldn't look at her.

No, you don't. You can't

Why not?

Because you don't love yourself.

Why?

Because you let me treat you just as bad as your father did.

He turned to me with eyes deep under his brow.

Do you know why we don't have any children?

I was scared.

Because her father fucked her so hard when she was a little girl that he ruined her insides. And now she's here in this miserable life with a miserable man. Did you know they lived in a nice big house with a clean lawn and a two-car garage when they were young?

Really scared.

Now, and for the last twenty years, she's lived in a trailer in the desert with a lunatic. I think it's time we did her a favor. Where is it?

He spun, bits flying from his mouth, his nub swinging, his eyes searching.

Oh, Don I do love you. I do. You know I do. But she was angry. She was pushing him.

Oh, my god, I'm dying.

I still don't know who said that.

He dropped to the floor. I laughed. I was really sacred now.

Auntie was frozen. Still his eyes were searching. She looked at me. That same halo from the morning was around her head again. But it wasn't the sun.

Son of a whore! Do you know your mother was a whore?

It didn't faze me. I'd heard it before. Though it did hurt a little.

Now, Don. Her hands were stretched out in front of her. Jesus she was glowing!

He looked over, but his hand was under the couch, searching.

Oh Don, Don. She smiled.

He found what he was looking for under me and in that same moment his face changed. To terror.

She was really glowing now and he was panicking. What did he see?

Her arms were out in front. Her eyes round and imploring. She looked light. I'm not sure her feet were on the floor.

Then he was up, the barrel propped on the stump, his fingers on the triggers.

You fucking devil!

All light. Fire. Explosion.

Silence.

And Auntie was gone. I couldn't hear and the window was smashed out. A little breeze came through.

He was up and out the window like a cat. The gun clunked to the hollow floor between us.

I came to the hole where the window used to be. He was there, over her, on the ground outside in the sun.

There were two big, bloody holes where her saggy breasts used to be. I remember him screaming. Laughing.

Now tell me of love God Damn It! Tell me. Please tell me!

I don't know how, but I heard her.

It is here. Always and forever.

And her life disappeared. Poof! In a flash. Gone.

And he was crying and laughing.

He knocked me over coming back through the hole in the wall, his eyes now just hollow. Gone. And the gun was reloaded, the triggers pulled, his grizzly head gone, sprayed on the ceiling. His body dropped to the floor and gun banged down beside him.

So tell me about love and I may laugh. Not in mockery though, in fear really.

* * * * * * * * * * * * * * *

Found at the scene of a murder/suicide outside Tempe, Arizona. Summer.

Eclipse, 1998

A Step Behind

What I'm going to tell you is private. Until now. I know. I'm making it public. But I want to. I think it's good. It's the right thing to do. I hope you can learn from my mistakes.

Beth and I were made for each other. And, like anything good, our meeting was unplanned, unexpected, miraculous, like the sunrise is miraculous. Inevitable.

I was walking past Penn Plaza on 34th street, on the sidewalk in front of the many benches. Usually there are bums on them, but today they were strangely empty. Except for her. She was there in long pants on a very hot day. Above the pants she had on a white shirt and sunglasses, which were black. Her brown hair was disheveled, flopped to the side. She looked dead. That's why I looked over, I guess. She was like a magnet. I had no choice.

Unconsciously, I stopped, clogging the foot traffic. As I did, and drew closer, her purse dropped off her lap and splattered open on the sidewalk. She was either dead or asleep. Or waiting with wide-open eyes hidden behind those dark sunglasses.

With the sound of her purse popping open, they came out—the bums—like leeches, like vampires, like hungry dogs.

Did I mention that she was beautiful? Right there, with the bums coming, the sun shining, she was perfect and I thought I might have to run away. But I couldn't. She was in danger and she didn't even know it. Maybe. At the time I thought for sure that the dark forces were rising against her and I had to act. I had to save her. Little did I know that those dark forces were nothing compared to the ones I would see in my time with her.

I dashed over and grabbed her purse. A few of the passers-by noticed but didn't do anything. New York is like that. Thankfully, the bums did see me and did withdraw back into the shadows of the Plaza. New York is like that too.

Just as I put her purse back together and set it down beside her on the bench, she slapped a hand down on my wrist. Her grip was a vice—iron hard. I saw heavy veins and thick, corded tendons flexing with pure strength.

"What are you doing?" Her voice, though tense, was a song to me.

"Your purse fell. I picked it up." My voice was surprisingly firm. I think she liked it.

Then she quickly snatched it away, yanked out a pack of cigarettes, and lit up. And smiled. Perfect white teeth. And when she slid off the sunglasses, she revealed the most amazing sea-green eyes I have ever seen. They were amazing because they were playful but hard, almost menacing, cat-like. I smiled too and happily breathed the cloud of cigarette smoke she blew in my face.

And that was it. What you're imagining is what happened. We hit it off, became friends, went out on dates. The usual. I was charming. She laughed and challenged me to think more. She opened up some. So did I. We had a relationship much like a montage in a movie. Always music and fun and laughter and kissing. We also rolled under the sheets many times. And many other places too. We enjoyed each other. We just had a lot of fun together. Filling up time was easy for us. We lived in the moment, dancing in life, so happy that we had found someone.

It turns out that she was asleep on the bench that sunny day because she had been up all night as a stand-in in a movie. She got to 34th street and literally collapsed from exhaustion. She loved acting and had high hopes for it. She would always explain to me with great energy about how movies were made and what she had done. It made her happy. I was happy to hear her talk.

—

The next event of any note between us happened six months into our relationship. Actually, it took place on our six-month anniversary.

At dinner in a nice place in the city, we sat opposite of each other and ate well. Afterward she was smiling and so was I.

"Six months. It's amazing these days." I reached for her hand. She let me take it.

"I like you because you make me laugh, yet you're so serious, so determined." I wouldn't have mentioned it, but it was out of character for her to talk that way. Stilted. Something was up. I just gave her a heavy sultry gaze and raised an eyebrow.

"What?" She was defending something. Her eyes narrowed. I let it go.

"Thanks. You're a sweet-heart to notice." I gave her hand a little squeeze.

"And you're so observant." Her eyes punctuated the remark by becoming tight green spots of light. Yes, something was definitely up. This was not cat and mouse. She wanted something. Or, maybe I did.

"I like your solidity. I like the fact that you're always the same. I count on that—on you. You're calm in a sea of chaos," she said.

Somehow our hand grips had changed and now she had me, tightly. But, I believed her. I liked what she said. My pulse quickened. I knew she was right.

She sighed deeply, low in her chest, and looked down. The room dimmed when I lost her eyes. She was trying to tell me something. Then she looked back up.

"Do you want to live here and do what you do, forever?" Her voice was less energetic, almost a rasp.

"No." I said too quickly. "Do you?" Again, too quick.

She looked away, across the room.

"No." She was insulted.

"You don't have to. You're so alive." I felt her grip loosen with my words so badly said. Still, her eyes were elsewhere.

"Are you thinking of going away?" My pulse picked up again.

"Not now. But, I don't want to be here forever." The words fell from her mouth like broken teeth. I looked at her neck: all tendons, strained, tight.

Then she looked up again. I knew she wanted to be my friend, to like me. I could tell she was trying very hard at that point.

"Don't you understand? I get lost if I stay in one place too long."

"Is that why you like acting?" It just came out, like a snake's tongue. Her eyes jumped wide at me, then turned away again. I realized she wasn't looking at anything so much as that she couldn't look at me.

"I guess so. Acting is the only thing I can do." Now she sounded defeated, flat and let go of my hand.

You have to understand though: she was beautiful. And part of her beauty, in that moment, was her conscious balance between being unbreakable and being so absolutely unguarded. And I realized also in that moment that she had very little idea of just how beautiful she was. I felt pity, but also, strangely excited. She showed me so much more than she could ever say. My finger tips tingled, the air grew sweet.

"Are you trying to tell me something?" I asked.

She looked up and hope flashed through her eyes and then vanished. She didn't like what she saw in me.

"Can we go?"

"You mean leave? Here?"

"Yes. I'm ready to go. Can we? Please?" And somehow, I had lost some notches on her respect meter.

"You don't have to ask permission." I smiled. She slowly slid her hand off the table and her eyes dropped.

And for the first time I saw something in her—from her— that in the coming months I would grow more accustomed to: total shutdown.

That night we limped through sex. I understand now that it was nothing more than momentum that got us through it. But, then, I still believed in it, in us, and enjoyed it though.

—

The next weeks—and into months—she threw herself into auditioning—something she had slacked away from as our relationship had grown. I saw her a lot less. I figured, dumbly, that it was a natural ebb in our relationship and that our passionate flow would soon return. So I plowed along as usual. Working. Slowly inching up the corporate ladder. I don't think about my job. It's not important to me.

I think she began to grow sick of me after an especially long week of fruitless auditions. She stomped into my apartment one night just as I was dozing on the couch. I shot straight up with the slam of the door.

"Too tall, too short, too hard, too soft, too hidden, too sexy, too homely! God-damned finicky little faggot directors! They don't know what the fuck they want! They say one thing and want another. And they don't explain anything! Completely irrational. Totally emotional. So stuck on themselves they can't give anyone else a chance! Want to do it all themselves! I am so sick of people telling me how I need to change!" She threw her keys across the room and stared directly at me.

I figured it best to remain silent.

Her eyes bored so far into me that I actually felt pain in the back of my head. I raised my brow and smirked trying to release the tension. In retrospect I see the mistake. But when you're in it, well, you're in it.

She went on.

"Am I fooling myself? Maybe I should just give up—give up my passion and be a damn drone!"

"Just like you," was right there in her glaring, blazing green eyes. I knew she stopped herself from saying it. I remained quiet, though I bet she saw a twinge of pain in the corner of my mouth, or the slight tightening of my shoulders.

I did love her, you know. I wanted to wrap her in comforting, accepting silence.

She wasn't having any of that though.

"There was this one guy, this director." She giggled wickedly as she turned away and paced, well, pranced, around the room, her neck straight and strong. "I met him on the street—he was a jerk—cocky—smart-assed, and he asked me—begged me—to come audition for him. I laughed in his face. Then he actually got on his knees. Can you believe it?"

Her eyes were silly with joy now. Obviously she wasn't seeing me anymore.

I don't know how to describe it, but, if, at that moment, I had stood up, walked over to her, grabbed her arm and slapped her, I know she would have grabbed me and hugged and hugged. I don't know why, but in that moment, when we were in it, it made more sense than anything. It was right there. And I would have hugged her back. It would have been, just so . . . what? Reasonable.

But, of course, I was silent. Cool.

This time she was too.

She turned and looked down at me, those green eyes wide, breathing heavily. This air-filled chasm opened between us.

"I love you," I could have said, but didn't.

She forcefully slowed her breathing with deep breaths that she held and then let out slowly through her nose. Maybe an exercise from her acting.

Then she smiled—not really in my direction. "Time to go night-night," and she sprang across the room on one, two leaps and through the door to my bedroom.

—

That night—later—in fitful sleep—her wrist smacked my nose and I jumped awake. I looked over, a dribble of blood inching down my lip. She was bare on the sheets and writhing. Her eyes were closed, yet fluttered wildly.

Then she was moaning. And her strong right hand clamped on her crotch. In that instant I wondered if she was really sleeping or just giving one hell of a performance. But I watched. I was riveted.

Her breathing raced through wide nostrils—hot sweat glistened on her flesh—her back arched—her elbow thumping in rhythm at her side—and it all grew, and grew and grew and BOOM! She exploded in a huge orgasm—a great, high wail, then rushing to exhale. My guts twisted and my tongue flicked across my bleeding lip while my fingers clenched. As she wound down, I thought to jump on her, but her breathing was slowing and her muscles relaxing as she drifted away with sweet, breathless content. What could I do? She was gone.

—

When we finally broke up, just two days later, and just shy of a year since I collected her scattered purse, she actually called me a bloodless fuck.

My mistakes weren't huge, but many. And their combined weight was what did me in. I never addressed her the way I should have. I was too busy being polite.

As much as she wanted to respect me, she couldn't because I was never what she wanted when she wanted it. I was too solid, too dependable, too even, I guess.

I was like her little science experiment, really. She looked down on me at the bottom of the bucket and poked at me and studied me and was fascinated for a while, but eventually grew bored of me and moved on. So, maybe I was made for her—for that. I don't know. It seemed like it at the time.

I saw her the other day—alone, asleep on a park bench— well, maybe asleep, with her purse busted open, scattered at her feet.

It was strange, I still wanted to help her, but knew I couldn't.

At Sunset, 1998

Shadows in the Sand

Once, when we were on the beach together, I noticed something about her that I had never seen before. Her shadow was perfect. Like a statue.

You see, a year before, I had wished for a goddess. I had wanted deliverance. And I got it.

The sun was setting behind the dunes, so its light was low and long. She and I were walking in the deep sand, not near the edge of the water, but in the heavy, hard-going stuff. We weren't close together. She was a couple of steps ahead. Her loose white shirt billowed out in front of me. Her hair blew behind. Golden. Lush.

Anyway, we're walking in the deep sand and it's a beautiful perfect sunset. The air is like a massage and the full, fresh scent of the ocean is delicious. The temperature is just right.

To anyone else, it would have been perfect.

But we're not touching, we're not talking, we're just trying to soak it up. Pores open. By that point we both needed to soak up something unquestionable, something real, uncontrived, like a beautiful sunset on the Outer Banks of North Carolina on the last weekend of July.

My skin was brown, salty and clean. My hair shifted in the wind and my nostrils were full with the freshest air on the planet. I felt the most alive I had in a long while. Maybe she felt the same way because her shoulders were low, untense, and she moved not unlike the sea oats on the dunes—fluidly in the wind, strong, yet lithe. God, just beautiful. She moved as I knew she could—as I remembered her moving when we first met. And in that moment I think she saw things very much the way I did: like we had stolen a moment of beauty from a world that wasn't ours anymore.

And that's really it. I knew this then, but I was too close to make any rational sense of it. We had both given up trying to make anything beautiful in our life together by that time and by giving up, by not trying, by being lazy and hateful, we had fallen out of love. I know now that being in love requires an awful lot of work and attention. And by that beautiful afternoon at the end of July, neither of us wanted to make the effort anymore.

We stopped, ankle deep in the warm sand. She turned and looked out over the sea. I was behind her and couldn't see clearly, so I stepped around her. When I did, I noticed my shadow emerge from hers on the sand. She was unaware, her eyes focused way out, in the distance, very far from me.

I stood beside her and just a bit behind. I thought it was very interesting at the time that I could take my arm and stick it into her side—the side of her shadow that is. I'm glad she didn't notice. I didn't want her to.

She stood tall and firm, like a tower, and I sniggered as I stuck first my finger, then my fist, then my whole arm right into her. She didn't feel a thing. But I did. I felt an obscene joy.

Then I reached out and up, made my arm into a spear, and stuck it right through her head. It was hilarious. I grabbed her throat and squeezed as tight as I could. I kicked out her knee caps, smacked her head, tore at her with long, menacing claws. And she never knew a thing. It was very cathartic for me. Then she turned and caught me in mid poke. But she was cool.

"Wow, look at you."

I instantly felt like a child. I knew she knew what I had been doing, what I had been thinking. What I wanted to do. She had this way of looking at me. Her head would tilt back, her chin would raise, like she was looking down at me. When she did that, her eyes changed. They became flat, unreadable. Usually, when her face was on a normal angle her eyes appeared big and round. Full. Hazel with mischievous gold flecks. That's one of the reasons I was so attracted to her, so long ago.

"You're all red. Flushed." She smiled without teeth.

I accepted early on that she was smarter than I was. But I had learned during our time together how to read her. Now this is not to say that I understood her. But I could at least tell the dominant emotion that was coming at me. Right at that moment I knew she was full of anger. When she said: "flushed", she wasn't even thinking about the color of my cheeks. This I knew.

"I was looking at your shadow," I said. I purposefully kept my face flat, expressionless, watching her.

She looked over her shoulder, making it clear that she thought I was an idiot. Then it came, the smile. Here we go.

"How interesting. Look. My shadow is tall, long, like a ribbon or a curtain maybe. Hey, look, yours is short, squat, like a stump." She pointed down.

"Or a steaming pile of shit," I thought.

My head-shadow was on the edge of the surf, the white foam was sinking right into the top of my billowing hair, swallowing it up, pulling it into the sea.

Just to spite me she pretended to become fascinated with our shadows and she stuck her arms out, lifted one leg, pulled her long hair way up. She did all sorts of silly, stupid things, just to spite me, just to make me feel stupid, to put me down, to keep me down.

I said nothing as the tide swished along the tops of my

shadow-ears and stood very still.

Of course she continued to ignore me and danced around and played like a child, always watching her shadow, dancing with her shadow. If I didn't know her so well, I'd think she was having fun.

I just watched her. I watched her jump and fly through the beautiful air. I watched her long, silken hair flowing behind her. I watched her strong arms and legs flexing and springing and bouncing. A moving sculpture. Kinetic. Real. Out of my reach. From another world. A world I had no business being in.

I turned away and watched my shadow in the surf. My head was gone now—the waves swallowing my shoulders.

"Hey, grumpy! Take those hands out or your pockets and do me a cart wheel!" She shouted.

She was moving up the beach—away from me, of course. She wanted me to dance for her, like a dog.

"OK, that was good, now roll over, play dead." She laughed. See what I mean?

Again, I was watching her, my heart skipping with every move. I mean, my god, she was just extraordinary. I loved to look at her. I could look at her all day. Just watch her. Not in a creepy way, not even in a sexual way, just watch . . . her. When she moved, even when she breathed, she was proof to me that God was strong, alive and well, and still the master of the shop. No question there. Anyone, and everyone, would agree. Even women, I think.

It was when we talked. That was the problem. That's obvious.

It was the magic hour—when everything is rich and heavy. The light was thick, like the air. The rolling surf was soothing, calming my heart. I looked up and down the beach and realized it was empty. It was all ours, we were all alone. It seemed appropriate. All of the other renters—the other happy couples—were up at their cozy houses making dinner, showering, playing games, having long, luxurious sex.

The wind picked up the loose sleeves of my white shirt and made them flap like sails. I slid my hands back into my pockets, sighed, and looked up the beach, back to her.

She ran up the side of a dune and stopped. Like the queen of the world she looked down on me, and the whole world. As much as I hate it, she just looked right up there. It made sense to see her way up, above, in the sunlight, especially from down here in the shadows, below. I knew I didn't deserve her. I never did. She was leaving and I was being left.

—

I looked back to the surf and my shadow. The foam was now sucking at my middle. I was half gone.

And my guts ached. They ached with longing—with need. We were in the perfect place for young lovers—at the beach, at sunset. Why couldn't it be like the movies? Even just for an evening? A moment? God, we were clean and young and alive and things were just fucked up. Why?

Maybe because six months ago I asked her to marry me and she said don't rush it, let it be. Because a year ago I crawled to her—crawled to her out of the remains of a good-old, down-home mental breakdown? I was wasted, worthless, deflated. Dead inside.

And then there she was. From the sky? And available. I couldn't believe it. I never could believe that she wanted me—just me. Who am I anyway? Nothing.

Of course she didn't know about my breakdown—even though I told her, she still didn't really know where I had come from.

And her—I'm her fourth boyfriend in two years—where is she coming from?

Three months ago we're in bed after wild sex and I'm telling her a story, and all I can talk about is death. Everything I say— everything I think of—in the story, leads the main character right to death.

Or a month ago she's quitting her job and laughing and saying she'll live off of me.

Or now, Jesus, there she is, on the dune, shining, beaming— stark fucking naked! And waiting. Athena.

She waved, shook her full breasts, blew kisses, and then ran down, across the sand, the sun on her back, to the water and dove into the crashing waves.

She slides through the waves like an animal, a sleek dolphin. Or a snake.

The surf is at my shadow-knees now. I am in the water. Well, my shadow is—in the water. But it's not the same water, or the same beach she just streaked across.

She swims toward me in the surf. I wonder what she sees. All I know is that every time her breasts peak out of the water I feel needles in my stomach—rusty long ones with barbs—fish hooks—old fish hooks—tearing me from the inside—like her.

"Come on! It's wonderful!" She laughed. And smiled. And cajoled.

Then she rolled over backwards—her slick belly and fine pubic hair slid under and her taut thighs followed—then her perfect feet. And sploosh! She's gone.

She's torturing me.

I have an erection that's twitching, straining, crying.

I must ravage her right here—and I could—she'd let me. But it wouldn't solve anything. She's happy to give me her body. And she's happy to take mine.

It's other exchanges that have killed us.

Eight months ago I ask her what she wants. She's already crying and flipping out about her, then, new job in retail.

"I dunno," she sobbed.

"You have to figure it out. It's the only way you'll find any happiness."

That just makes her sob harder. She's naked, hunched over on my bed.

She blew her nose into a T-shirt and dropped it.

"What I want is for you to make some money to support us."

I stroked her head.

"I will."

Her eyes shot up. They burned hot through the haze of tears.

"Really?"

"Well, yeah, I've got to do something. I love you. I want to be with you always. It's simple."

She held her breath. Her fingers dug into a pillow in her lap.

"OK," she sighed.

And that was it.

—

Now she's naked in front of me, coming out of the water, like the fleshy version of the ocean itself—a human wave of heavy water, pushing and strong—rising up—emerging like

Athena out of Zeus' head. Broad, strong shoulders. Straight jaw, tight waist, plump breasts, long legs, and just oozing sex. Hot in the low sunlight. I ached. I hurt. I wanted to die right there—in her full, naked gaze. Right there. Dead. Please kill me.

But, she's coming to me and I'm afraid. Be careful what you wish for. Shit, I know it's over.

Her eyes are dead on me as she walks over the last bit of my shadow in the sand. The gold flecks were glowing in her eyes, mesmerizing. Like a predator.

Her real toes sank into my shadowy-shins—all that was left of me. And with pure lust, pure heat, pure rage, pure sex she came right up to me. I was terrified. She knew. She had always known.

Then she's kissing me, deeply, fully, while rubbing my completely mindless hard-on.

I am dead.

And she moves around me—past me—her hand trailing across my chest—fingers tipped in nails scraping—over me— then, gone, slinking back into the shadows of the dunes, behind me, in front of the sun. Now her shadow overlaps me. When she passes I feel the sun go cold on my back.

I'm left staring out to sea. It's minutes from darkness.

I feel something in my throat—something she has left in there for me with a kiss.

I swallow, but it won't go down. My nose runs, my eyes are dripping, and from way down, I sob. It's the last breath that will ever mean anything to me.

Now night has come. She has evaporated back into the darkness and I am frozen on the edge of the sea—not a man, not me, not anything—not even a shadow in the sand.

an autumn's eve, 1993

Anniversary

"I'm sick. I know it."

Anne watched her husband across the breakfast table, her eyes lean.

Mark looked well enough to her. His beard was thick yet cleanly trimmed around the good angles of his face. His eyes showed a little panic, way back. She wasn't used to seeing them without his glasses in front. Now, in the soft morning light, they looked smaller, like small spots on his face.

His color was good, not pale or yellow or grey. No, his color was fine. Even though she'd heard him say that he was sick so many times before, she still checked him over, just in case.

"Do you feel weak? Should you stay home from work?" Anne tried to sound concerned.

"No. I've got to work. It is a beautiful day though. It would be nice to sit on the porch. Just sit in the sun with a pitcher of ice tea and a book." He paused. The light in his eyes faded. "No. I can't stay home."

Mark shuffled the loose morning paper away from him and down to the seat of the empty chair between them. He looked at his wife. Her long black hair framed her face so well.

"Do you feel sick?" he asked.

"Not at all. I feel great."

Anne jumped up with her empty cup and plate and walked over to the sink. She looked through the white curtain over the window, outside. The driveway was empty. The car was in the garage. Fuzzy birds dropped from the tree next to the black driveway and flew away. She wondered if birds ever got sick.

Mark joined her at the sink. With a flash she thought how he must have been moving extra slow to invite any malady that might float by.

He placed his plate and mug beside hers in the sink.

She turned away to the toaster and wiped some crumbs off the counter in front of it. She heard Mark rinse his cup and then refill it from the tap. She imagined the up and down motion of his Adam's apple as he chugged down the water.

"The water will help. You can never drink too much water," she said as she turned around to face him.

He placed the empty cup in the sink and wiped his lips with his shirt cuff.

"You're right. It'll flush it out."

She looked at him. He looked at her.

His eyes again showed panic, way in the back.

"What are you doing today?" he asked. She never saw his mouth move. Her eyes stayed on his.

"Errands. Nothing special." She walked away to the round kitchen table. There she picked up the jelly jar and the cream container.

He watched her with distant eyes, could feel the sickness brewing in him, and wondered where it would strike first.

"Maybe you should see a doctor after work." She closed the refrigerator door.

"Maybe. I doubt he'll tell me anything. These things are hard to pinpoint," he said as he crossed the small kitchen to his chair to get his jacket.

"I guess you're right," she said, crossing the small distance back to the sink.

As he slid into his jacket, Mark had a stray thought: "Maybe the silent thief cancer is lurking somewhere in me." He sighed loudly.

"I'm not worried about it," he said as he collected his briefcase and then slid on his glasses.

Anne turned again to look at her husband. His eyes were dead on her. She was shocked. Her stomach twitched.

"Good. If you worry, you'll only make it worse." Quickly she picked up the dish towel and wiped her hands.

Mark sighed again. He was feeling weaker by the moment. He looked at his wife. Silhouetted by the light from the window she looked like a paper doll.

"Maybe we should have dinner tonight," he quietly suggested.

"That would be nice." Anne dropped the towel and followed his back to the front door.

He turned his hand on the knob.

"A good dinner would make me feel a lot better. I'm sure." He looked down at Anne and saw the corners of her straight mouth point up in a small smile.

"It would make me feel better too." She tipped up on her toes and pecked his cheek.

Mark sighed one last time, touched his wife's arm with his free hand, and stepped through the door.

Once the door was closed Anne walked back to the sink. Mechanically she turned the water on and rinsed the dishes. As her husband's car motored past the curtained window, she looked down to his cup in her hand. It didn't need to be rinsed, but she did it anyway, rubbing the rim under the stream from the tap. As she did, she thought about how much a good dinner wouldn't do a God-Damned thing for either of them.

Poke, 2003

The Evil Eye

It was on a Sunday, when it happened.

We'd been there—the bamboo forest—hundreds of times before. It was our battleground. Our playground. Our secret place to have fun.

We both had our outfits—green rubber army boots and coats with pockets full of important things—walkie-talkies, twine, knives, matches, paper and pens for drawing the battle plans. Everything.

We were well equipped. We knew what we were doing.

"The Germans are right over there," he whispered, pulling me to the ground.

I checked my gun and flattened myself.

"They've got a big gun and grenades." He looked at me. "How many you got?"

I checked one of my pockets. I had four magnolia cones.

"Four."

"Good. So do I." He smiled.

Then he pulled one out, snapped off the stem and threw it out in front of us.

"BOOM!" He yelled.

"Two more, and we go." His eyes were intense. This was very real for him.

We each snapped a stem and heaved them ahead.

"BOOM! BOOM!" "Now go. GO!"

He jumped up and ran forward chattering his teeth like a

machine gun.

I followed.

"BAM! BAM!," I yelled, my pistol out in front.

Then he was hit.

"AAARRRGGGHHH!" He grabbed his belly and fell down in front of me, sprawled.

I dropped down and scooted over the broken bamboo shoots to him.

"That's it. I'm dead. You're a good soldier. Thanks."

His eyes fluttered. His body shook wildly. Then he went limp.

I watched him.

Then he jumped up.

"What we need is a fort."

I stood up beside him.

"They'll never get us then." He marched around. "That's how we beat the Germans."

His eyes searched the ground.

"All right. Go get some of those logs over there."

He pointed to a pile of fallen bamboo.

I ran over, grabbed and arm load, and came back.

He was already digging a hole with a stick. I set the pile down beside him.

"Footings," he said over his shoulder, "and we need some rope."

I pulled a ball of twine out of one of my pockets.

"Good." He took it.

Then he shoved one of the brittle bamboo stalks in the ground.

"Get the cross piece," he ordered.

I picked up one of the old husks.

"Give me the end."

I did and he began furiously tying it to the shaky upright.

"Now, set the other post."

I took another rotten piece of bamboo and shoved it into the opposite hole in the ground. Then he raised the end.

"Tie it off." He tossed me the twine and I did as he said.

Now we had a cross piece.

He marched around, touching it, hitting it—to check its strength.

It rattled and squeaked with his blows.

"Perfect."

It was about three feet off the ground.

Then he dragged over a stack of husks.

"What are you doing?" I asked.

"Got to test it."

He put a foot up on the shaky pile. Then another.

They rolled right from under him and he flew forward— arms out—and snapped through the cross piece and landed heavily.

Neither of us moved.

"Shit! Shit! They really got me now!"

I rushed around and saw the blood.

"Oh my god."

A piece of the bamboo had snapped, stuck in the ground, and jammed into his eye.

"Oh my god," I said as he rolled over.

Blood just washed down his face.

"Shit!" He jumped up, grabbed the piece with both hands and yanked it out.

What was left of his eyeball came out and hung down on his right cheek. He quickly wiped his hand across the blood there.

I was light-headed and shaky. My chest was fluttering.

"Jesus," I whispered.

But he stood firm and looked from his bloody hand to me.

"They got me good this time."

—

His parents were calm about the whole thing.

They drove him to the hospital and waited patiently while he was treated.

I showed up with my folks just as he was being wheeled to the elevator.

"Is he all right?"

His mom limped over. She'd always had a limp. I think she liked it.

She was fat, her dress over-sized. Her hair was a mess.

She kept rubbing her hands.

His father—a bear of a man—stood silently behind. Scary. Imposing.

"Yes. He'll be fine. He'll get a glass eye of course."

I swear she smiled.

"No other damage."

His father harumphed.

Then he was wheeled by. His eye—or where it had been— was under a gauze patch. He was smiling.

"You came through unscathed."

I moved close and walked along with the gurney.

"Yes."

"Yes." Something was different. He was far away.

"Are you OK?"

"Oh, yes. I will be." He sounded like an old man. My intestines tensed and my knees locked.

And he was gone into the elevator.

———

They took out the damaged parts and fitted him with a glass eye. Same color. Same shape.

It just didn't move.

When he looked to the side, it always stayed right on you. It was spooky. It looked so real, but didn't act that way.

I felt like he, or it, was always watching.

———

He was spending more time at home. We were together less.

I called him. Sometimes he called back.

———

One day I saw him in town with his father.

They were eating ice cream. I only mention it because it never had happened before.

"Hey." I waved.

We stopped in front of each other. His father looked like a big kid standing behind him totally consumed with his ice cream.

The damn eye was right on me. His other eye was looking

past me, up the sidewalk.

"Hey." He said between licks.

"What's up?"

"Dad and I are going to a baseball game."

"Great." I hoped he'd ask me to go. I really thought he would.

"OK. See you later."

They walked right by me. His father never looked at me.

I was left alone on the street.

"I don't understand."

My mom looked at me from across the dinner table and smiled sympathetically.

"Families close their ranks after a tragedy. To heal."

"But they seem so happy about it."

"Tragedies bring people together too."

"No. I mean like they're glad it happened."

"No, I don't think so." She frowned.

Maybe she was right. All I knew was I saw him less.

One day I went over to his house like I used to.

I rang the bell and his mother came to meet me.

She stayed on the other side of the screen door.

"Hi. Is he here?"

"He's with his father," she chimed. Her eyes were distant. Evangelical.

"Could I see him?"

"He's out back with his father."

She closed the door.

What the hell was going on?

I walked around the house to the fence.

They were about half-way through building a brand new tree fort.

The lumber was stacked neatly. The nails. The glue. A big saw set up on a table in the sun.

They were working together. I watched him hold up a 2x4 while his dad hammered it in place.

Then he saw me. He said something to his father who looked over and then looked away.

The eye was on me as he strolled over. It was stabbing into me. Like a knife. Like bamboo.

"Need some help?" I asked.

"No."

I actually felt physical pain. In my chest.

"Oh. OK," I mumbled.

Silence was firmly wedged between us like a battleship. I could feel it pushing on me.

"I don't want to be your friend anymore."

"What? Why?" I cried.

"I don't like you anymore. You let me down on the battlefield."

"What?"

He looked down, but that eye was right there.

"You pushed me."

"What!?"

The eye. Like a diamond. Like a drill. Like an ice pick jammed in my head.

His voice had been even. He wasn't angry. His arms were at his sides. He was completely calm.

Then he turned and walked away.

I ran all the way home.

"But I didn't mom. You've got to believe me. I didn't push him!" I sobbed.

She wrapped me in big, warm arms.

"I'm so sorry."

"He's the one that did it!"

"I know. I believe you."

I liked being in her arms.

"Best to let it go," she whispered.

"What? Just like that?" I buried my head in between her arm and breast. Warmth.

"There's nothing you can do. His mind is made up."

She squeezed me and I sobbed and sobbed and sobbed. She worked me like an accordion, squeezing the pain out of me until it was over.

Even after it was over.

Negative Landscape Four, 1994

A Hole in the Ice

I remember it so well, that day I fell through the ice, when I was a boy.

I was out alone in the early morning. The light through the trees was like God smiling. Everything was bright and white and crisp and clean. The air was perfect and clean, cold and invigorating.

It was strange though, how quiet it was. For a second I wondered if all the birds had left, or were dead.

The pond near our house was a wide expanse of white—much bigger than a football field. My head was bare, but the rest of my body was wrapped in layers of warmth. My heavy boots crunched into the ankle-deep snow as I approached the edge of the pond. I was happy to be there, happy to be alive on that perfect, clear day.

My mother had always said that heaven was whatever you wanted it to be. On that crisp, bright morning I knew I wanted heaven to be just like that.

I had been on the ice before, earlier in the winter. The pond had frozen and there was no snow. The ice was like thick glass—a natural wonder of strength and beauty. My father and I had skated on the pond for a week before it had warmed up.

He liked to skate at night. He would cut circles in the reflected moonlight. The slicing of his blades would make the ice sing. It was so quiet out there that I would often just stop in the middle, in the wide glow of the moon and listen to my heartbeat throbbing in my throat. And then my dad would fly by, a wide smile on his face and his long scarf blowing behind him.

After we finished and were exhausted we would lie on our backs in the middle of the pond and look for shooting stars. We rarely talked—mostly just to point out one of the quick, bright streaks in the sky.

I will carry those nights with me for the rest of my life.

———

That morning, when I was alone at the pond, I knew the ice was questionable. Dad had always said two things about snow on ice: "One, it ruins the surface for skating. And two, it's like a blanket and it warms the ice, making it dangerous."

At eight years old I couldn't quite grasp that idea. Snow was cold. Ice was cold. How would it make the ice warmer? What I watched for was the sun. It hadn't yet made it over the pond. It was still low that morning, shining through the trees.

Still, I was careful. I took a tentative first step. Near the edge, the ice was strong. It held me up easily. So I inched out further—sliding my feet through the snow. It felt fine and I was light, probably only fifty pounds at that age.

So I continued out, slowly sliding my feet, to the middle. I looked up just as a flock of geese honked over head. They must have been looking for a place to land.

Maybe the ice cracked at that point. I don't really know. Anyway, it gave, and I went through, in and under.

My heavy boots pulled me right down to the bottom. Swiftly, like rocks.

I didn't panic. Maybe, somewhere deep in me, I knew it was going to happen—sooner or later—so maybe I was prepared.

I wasn't cold immediately. I couldn't see anything. It was very dark under there—like death dark.

I landed on the bottom and my boots sank right into the mud. I reached down and unlaced them and slipped out with little trouble. Then I tried to swim up, but the water was thick and heavy. My jacket was full, so I slid it off. I had swimming lessons the summer before, so was OK, for the moment. I looked up and it was like the sky was a lid. It was beautiful though—soft and glowing—muted, soft light, up above. All was silent.

Way up there was a dark spot though—a hole in that soft, blanket sky—a hole in the ice. It stunned me. It was ugly, horrible, a blemish in that beautiful blanket—the top of the world, holding me and all this darkness down in here. I hated it and knew that it would bring ruin on me if I went to it. But something deep in me told me that I had to, that I had to get to it. I had to get to that ugly, black hole and climb back into that world.

My jacket fell away and I was struggling up, up to that hole. I pushed against nothing in my void there, legs spreading out wide, pumping, and grabbed at even less with my hands and arms. I wasn't getting any closer. For a moment I thought I was staying, and that didn't seem too bad. But that black hole loomed, hateful, laughing in a sucking way.

Around that time I realized I was cold—my skin—icy water down in my ear canals—my feet . . .

But my lungs were on fire. And not good fire. It was a fire that wanted to be quenched—a fire that longed to die.

They say that's probably when I lost consciousness. I don't

know. Things did slow down, the dark water around me was thick. It was all so calm though. I could have been dreaming the whole time.

The thing I will always remember is seeing that black hole in the beautiful, soft blanket, lid-sky and knowing that the life on the other side was mine, like it or not.

—

My father must have been nearby. Maybe he was coming to join me by the pond. They say I was under for a good ten minutes and that I lost consciousness about half way through.

He later told me that he stripped down nude and shimmied out through the snow, on the ice, on his belly. When he got to the hole he watched for any movement. Then he was in. He swam straight down and, somehow, found me. Then he pulled me up to the surface. He was a strong man.

He slid me up on the ice. It broke and I was sinking again. He swam down, grabbed me again and pushed me up, again. Every time he would get me on the ice, it would break again and we moved toward the bank a few feet at a time this way. Since it was already broken, it was so much easier for it to just keep breaking.

I wonder what he was thinking and feeling. I'll never know because I never thought to ask. Until now.

He finally got me on the ice when we were ten feet from the edge and he could stand up. Then he pushed me to land—slid me across the top then, through the snow.

On the shore, he pumped my chest and got the water out. I can't imagine how cold he was. Then he wrapped me in his jacket, picked me up, and ran us through the snow back to our house. I guess along the way the jostling made me cough and the rest of the water came out.

—

The next thing I remember is being in water again—floating—but this time I was warm and breathing. When I opened my eyes I saw my mother staring down at me. Her large brown eyes were full of concern. I knew she knew I was all right, but there was something else bothering her. It was small, but I knew it would grow. Dread. Somehow I felt like my falling in the ice was a catalyst for something else in her, something ugly, something hateful, like a black hole in the sky. Her deep eyes said that so clearly. I laid still. She reached down and ran a warm, wet cloth over my forehead. She wanted to save me, but dad had already done that.

I wondered where he was. Then I saw his arm beside me—under me—supporting me. I turned my head and there he was, right under me in the bathtub. My back was resting on his chest. This kept my head up so I could breathe, but still be surrounded by the warm bath water.

"Thank God," my mother whispered. She grabbed my cheeks and kissed my head. "Thank you dear, sweet Jesus," she sang.

I must have smiled because she smiled at me. But not in her eyes. Only her mouth smiled, her eyes were still worried.

I felt dad kiss the back of my head and squeeze my arm. Then mom wrung out the wash cloth, laid it flat on the edge of the tub, and walked out.

They got a doctor to come anyway—to check me over. He said I was lucky—no damage. I agreed. I didn't feel damaged, just different. Something was different. An image of the trail of broken ice came into my mind. I could see it—a jagged line from the center of the pond to the edge of the shore. And then that black hole.

—

Soon after I noticed my parents talking less, being less close, and arguing more. The house was always cold. Even when spring came and the beautiful ice and snow melted away and beautiful bright flowers replaced them, the house still held a chill.

The geese returned and by summer they were escorting their new fuzzy, yellow babies all over the pond. I would sit on the vibrant green hill nearby and watch them for hours.

I was rarely at home that summer. I found myself attracted to the pond. I felt I had no choice. I had to go there. Though it seemed so simple, something major had happened there. My falling through the ice last winter had meant something— something I couldn't understand. And as I sat there begging the pond and the sky and the trees to tell me something I wondered if I was asking the right questions. They all responded only with the breeze, or a gentle lapping at the edge or with bright white clouds slowly drifting away. The white of those clouds mocked me, like the snow on that day. They mocked me in silence and I often found myself crying on the bank of the pond, screaming at the sky, sobbing hopelessly, my tears sinking into the dark earth.

I noticed that when the three of us were together, things were hard—like swimming through the thick winter water when I was under the ice—pushing against nothing—lots of pushing and lots of nothing. None of the carefree joy was with us anymore. None of the simple beauty that had made the family work was around either. It was just cold.

Dad was quiet. Mom slammed things on tables and windows and doors. I knew it was my fault. What had taken our life away? How could something so harmless do so much damage? Nobody died. Nothing bad happened, yet it was like a bomb went off in our house and the three of us were blown to different corners of the world. And we didn't know how to get back. And there was just this . . . what?, I don't know, sadness. Everywhere. All the time.

Now that I'm older I realize that my mother blamed my father for what happened, and my father, at first, blamed himself too. But later he began to blame her, to blame her for not trying to get back—for not trying to rebuild the us of a family. He was so consumed with blaming her, and she with him, that after a year we all knew it was impossible to ever get back what had been lost by my falling through the ice.

I realize these things happen—that this is what life is all about—how we deal with things like this. Now I realize this. But then I couldn't figure how I not only knocked a hole in the ice that day, but how I knocked a hole in my family too.

Walk Alone, 1994

A Clean House

Can only God forgive? I mean, really FORGIVE?

I'd like to think not. Unfortunately, my hopes are continually and thoroughly kicked into the proverbial gutter.

It's not that I ask much. Just a kind eye, or a turning away, maybe.

Sure, I killed a few animals when I was a kid. Who didn't? It wasn't wrong. It was forgivable. Do you think God forgave me? I didn't have to eat them, but I did. Like the Indians. Did God forgive them? I really don't think God thinks those things are bad. But people do, and God damn them! Animals eat other animals. They have to. Life requires some amount of violence. Right? And forgiveness. I mean it.

If somebody held your nose—held you down—with some friends—so you couldn't breathe—what would you do? Take it?

No sir, you wouldn't.

And if somebody kicked you down into the street, with traffic coming right at your head, and laughed—or worse—just walked away, what would you do?

Or if when you're a little kid some dirty dog kicked you on the ground and peed on you, what would you do? Forgive them? Would you? Really?

Like this time this little old woman—a picture of geriatric beauty—fucked me. Not like you're thinking. She was my landlady. I lived in her basement.

It was nice. Cozy. Dark during the day. Good shutters.

They locked tight. My own bathroom. Closets. Fully furnished. Just like home.

It even had a big floor rug. She told me it was old. Persian. But I thought it was beautiful—like her—like everything in her house. Yes, old and beautiful, like her, like her house.

But, I digress.

Now I'll tell you how she fucked me.

I had just paid my rent. Fall was beginning. Things were good. I felt very invigorated. Alive. Full of life. Unafraid. Very able. Capable. Super-duper.

One night I came home. I tidied up a little. I always kept the place really clean. And I hear her moving around upstairs. It was late. Too late for her. Her flat slippers were nervously slapping on her wooden floors. It was maddening. Driving me crazy.

Then she stopped. By the phone. I'm very smart and only having seen her place once, or twice, I had the layout memorized. When she's over my bathroom, she's on the phone.

I listened. Held my breath. She was dialing. Then whispering. Then whimpering into the phone. I have a sense about things and I knew something was not right. What was her problem?

Then she shuffled away, upstairs, and quietly closed her door. What was she afraid of? Did she not want to wake me? Was she afraid I'd hear her? I forgave her for her fear. It wasn't hard. She was old. And beautiful. Like a mother.

Then I heard the bed springs squeak. But the lights were on. I could see them shining into the yard, out through the cracks in my shutters. So, she wasn't going to bed. She was waiting for something.

I don't know how long I stood there breathing in little sips—trying to be silent—and listened.

Then I heard it, or them. In the distance. Getting closer. And I knew they were coming for me. Flashing lights coming up the road. I could feel the energy, you know?

Everything changed. The world went red and I was running for the back door. But it was locked. I never locked the back door.

So out the front I went, low to the ground. I had to get away. I skimmed the grass, sprinting away from her house. But, once I was to the street . . .

"Freeze!"

I was terrified. Blue lights were flashing everywhere. Shadows under hats were yelling at me. Black guns in the night were pointed at me.

I froze.

"On the ground! NOW!"

I just dropped. His words were bullets in my chest.

They rushed forward and put their dirty hands on me, their knees in my back. And then handcuffed me. I had no control.

As I strained to lift my head, I saw her coming out on the stoop. For a moment our eyes were locked together. She was sobbing. I knew she felt bad for what she did to me. She was begging me to forgive her and at the same time trying to forgive me. I could see it as plain as day. I felt an angry hand rustle me up and shove me forward, toward her. Little did they know that all that would—or could—be said between us was already taken care of. Idiots.

She led us, the whole silly posse of us, around the back of the house. And as the lights died away behind us, blocked by her house, I felt a strange flutter in my chest. Quite against my will I approached the back shed and saw something out of place, on the ground. She stopped ten feet from it and pointed with a hand over her mouth. She could go no further. That was her limit. I forgave her that too.

The cops pulled out their flashlights and shined them down on the mound. A few of them stayed back with the lady and a couple others pushed me toward it. This one stinking dirty bastard cop made me look down. I knew what was there.

"Christ!" He sputtered. "Go get a shovel."

Then he just stared at me.

"Ma'am, would you like to wait inside?"

No. She whimpered. The tears were really rolling now. Still, I couldn't believe she was doing this to me. I had done us—BOTH OF US—a favor.

Women. I can even forgive God for them.

So this other fat, huffing cop finally comes back with a shovel and starts digging into the mound. The shovel made sick slicing sounds in the damp dirt.

"Please, be careful." She whimpered again.

He slowed down. Like there was something valuable under there. It was all for show. For her. So, I even forgave that cop for trying to be nice, even when it really did not matter one little bit. I looked at the other cop watching the one digging. His eyes were wide. I could tell he was scared and excited at the same time.

It didn't take long before he found it. Then he started digging with just his hands. He scooped away the black earth until it was uncovered. And there it was. That same stupid grin was still on its face. The old lady collapsed. The cop gasped showing how much of a light-weight he really was.

"What?" I asked.

He hit me across the face. Yes, he did. I still can feel the sting. Maybe God will forgive him. Not me.

We were all frozen there for a minute.

"That thing shit on my—YOUR—antique rug!"

She looked over at me from the ground. This time her eyes were searching mine like fingers inspecting your privates.

I just didn't understand. Why me? Why all of this?

And then a strange thing happened. I had a feeling I don't think I've ever had before: sadness. That woman loved her dog. She was going to be lonely without it. But, if she had just been more forgiving, she might have had my company a little longer too.

I couldn't help it. I started laughing. Low and dirty. Into the dirt. The cop kicked me in the side. I rolled over.

"All this for a dog!"

"What?!" He was reeling. Because he was weak.

"Just what do you think this is?"

He pointed down into the hole at that stupid smiling face. What an idiot.

"A dog, of course. Are you blind? Kind of looks like a retriever we had once."

They all just stared at me with wide eyes, their jaws slack.

Then they panicked. They yanked me up yelling unintelligibly and pushed me back out of the yard to their flashing cars and threw me in. I don't think they even helped the woman up.

Then I was in jail, in court, and in jail again.

Why I'm in jail for killing a dog, I don't know. It was a good thing. The right thing.

And why these people come in here and ask me questions about my childhood and anger and stuff, I don't know either.

The damn thing was a nuisance! No respect! Always licking her, kissing her, trying to be my friend. Trying to talk to me.

Like today—this guy—a doctor I guess—asked me about my old lady.

"How do you think she is?"

"Like I care."

"Do you think she misses Henry?"

"What, the dog?"

He just stared.

"She had a funeral for that dog."

I laughed in his face.

"What?"

"Yes, your whole family was there."

He was trying to spook me. I could tell because his eyes were all big behind his thin glasses.

I showed nothing.

"My family's dead, Doc. I told you."

"What about your mother?"

"Lives alone in the city."

"Where are you from?"

"The country. The trees. The mud. Not here."

"What about your father?"

"Ran away when I was a kid. I told you that already."

"What would you say if I said you were lying?"

"I'd try to forgive you. I like you."

"Your father was recently killed. Did you know?"

Probably stealing something or playing cards.

"Somebody killed him with a shovel. Beat him to death and buried him in the back yard."

Oh, I was laughing on the inside. These Docs are always trying to trick you. He was trying to make me feel sorry for the old woman and her dog by telling me how my daddy died. Wanted me to feel bad about it. Wanted me to think the dog was my dad and I killed him like the piece of shit he was.

"Why are you crying?" he asked.
"I'm not. It's dry in here."
It was.

Forgiveness is funny thing. Only God can do it right. You understand what I'm saying?

Cyclops, 1997

Interludes

(down the pipe)

Hollywood, 1993

Hand in Hand

And the strangest thing was that without a word she sat beside me on the bench.

Comfortably.

And immediately I was staring.
Maybe it was my eyes, because in her eyes
was trust.

It was just another moment in her day, her life, when she sat. Just as when she scooted closer to me.

She knew what I intended to do because I was staring at them—her feet—beneath her long, heavy skirt. They were dirty from abandoning her shoes blocks ago. She just left them.

Her feet were strong, well shaped, under the grime.

She smiled

and stretched her legs out in front and

flexed her toes,
spreading them wide. There was grime in between as well.

So I stood and offered her my hand. She smiled,

dipping her chin,
and took it.

And we were walking the two blocks to my house,

hand in hand.

Only touching. Not looking. The spring air was refreshing,
the air moving, warm. And full.

And, then, we were there.

———

In my bathtub I'm checking the heat with my fingers under
the running faucet.
She's sitting on the edge, her skirt pulled up to her knees.

Then the water was right.

I took her feet and tenderly placed them under the flow.
The water was brown, heavy with dirt, as it spiraled down
the drain.

I turned the soap in my palms.

And lathered her feet. Especially inbetween her toes. My
fingers in. My thumb a perfect fit in her arch. The soap and
warm water there.

Then the water ran clean. And her eyes came up to mine.

And she pushed them down flat on the tub as the water ran over.

I noticed her smile—

I think because the water was warm.

And for a second . . .

a glorious second . . .

I rinsed her feet again—my palms gently sliding over the tops, my thumb slowly down her big toe to the nail, and fingers cupping underneath. The tips of my fingers in the spaces between her toes. Underneath. Each. Space.

—

And then it was time. I squeezed her feet and then let them go and turned off the water.

She lifted her legs and moved on the edge of the tub and I caught her pristine feet with the softest towel I had and rubbed and dried them. Then I lowered them to the floor.

And she stood.

Straighter.

And smiled again.
I led her out of the bathroom.

Then I saw my new brown boots—just broken in—by the door.

Above them, she slipped one, then the other, bare foot in. I smiled.

The boots were good. They would last.

I slid the bolt back,
touched her hand lightly,
and led her to the street above.

There, I took a liberty and slid my hand around her head,

by her ear,

into her thick hair and

squeezed lightly the muscles of her taught neck.

In the warm sunlight.

Her chin dipped. She saw the boots,

then raised her glorious shining eyes to mine.

Smiled.

Turned.

And in that moment I knew love.

I knew surrender.

Then she looked up the way, focused in front of her, and walked up the street—away—her long skirt swaying over the tops of my boots, now hers.

I watched her for a block, though I could have watched longer.

Cloister's Window, 1999

A Few Words from Our Sponsors

Jimmy was walking down the street on a particularly bright summer afternoon. His bare feet padded the hot concrete. His loose hair hung off of his shoulders like a lion's mane.

He punched the first kid he saw that day. It was a friend of his that he put all of his anger into.

He continued walking, leaving the bleeding boy in his past. His face had no expression as he rounded the corner of the street. His hands hung limply at his sides.

Jimmy turned at the end of the block to cross the street and never saw the truck that smacked into him so hard that his teeth fell out.

—

"I like you a lot." He blandly stated. His tie was askew and his lip was bleeding.

"If you like me so much then why don't you ask me out on a date?" she replied leaving her lips slightly parted as if to invite a bloody kiss.

"Give me a minute to clean up the rest of this street trash and I will," he said noticing her parted lips. "I'll be with you in just a minute."

He continued beating the men with his stick.

When he was done, he wiped his mouth and approached her.

"Now how about that date honey?" he asked while straightening his tie.

She looked at him sheepishly. Her eyes were moist with adoration.

"Well, where would you like to go then?" she asked quietly.

He looked into her eyes and said, "how about my room? It's just upstairs."

She took his arm and let him lead her away from the alley.

In the morning she dressed quickly and quietly. She scribbled a short note and left his room.

When he woke he found the note on the dented pillow next to his. It said: "Thank you for my last night of wonder. I will never see you again."

He crumpled the note in his bruised hand and tossed it into his cheap, plastic trash can.

———

A woman stood in her empty apartment. She looked at the blank walls and the vacant floors and wondered why her husband had taken the children and left her all alone.

"Before we go kids we're going to have to flush the fish." He said happily. "Your mom will be home soon so hurry up flushing. I know you don't want to lose your pet. But he won't survive the trip to the other side of the world," he laughed.

That morning he hid behind the bathroom door. She came in to freshen up before she went to work for the day. She couldn't figure where he was.

She left the kid's lunch money on the counter in the kitchen and sighed as she left the apartment.

—

The wind swept the sand up into swirls. The wide brim of her straw hat caught some of the sand as it blew by. She brushed the lose grains away with her sharp, red-tipped fingers. Her oversized black sunglasses slid down her oiled nose as she lowered her hand. Her arm jingled her lose jewelry as she flicked some excess off of her darkly tanned legs. She unbuttoned the front of her inflated bikini top to release her small, pointy breasts to the sun. They were pale on her chest. She dripped some oil onto top of her pink nipples. The oil glistened in the sunlight, full of heat, full of light. She slowly rubbed her breasts with the oil and then pinched a nipple between her fingers. She laughed as she thought about fucking. She laughed instead of crying because she hadn't fucked in a long time.

—

Control is never taken, only given away. I knew this entirely too well when she slid her arm across my shoulders that night—the night we met.

It was a subtle gesture. She probably didn't even think about it. But I know on that night, in that moment, with that gesture, I had lost. It was over. Now all we had to do was play it out.

We met on a rainy Sunday afternoon in the early fall. The air was just getting chilly. I was content—not happy mind you—but content.

And she just materialized.

I had my whole face in a book—DeSade, I think. And all of a sudden, there she is right beside me.

"Hi," she said.

"So where did you come from?" I pushed DeSade aside, giving her my full attention.

She laughed. Delicately. Nicely.

"That would take a long time to answer."

I liked her immediately. Playful.

I smirked, fiddled with my lighter.

"No, no, I mean, how long have you been here? I usually notice everything. I never saw you sit."

"I just sat with my coffee. Maybe you're not as perceptive as you think." Again grinning. Like a cat.

Then she turned toward me revealing her beautiful breasts that had been concealed under her big rain coat.

I looked right at them. She knew. She had used that trick before—and would again.

"So, what brings you out on this rainy Sunday?"

"A sense of adventure." She smirked again. She had me.

"You don't come here much, do you?"

"Why? Do you come here a lot?" She crossed her arms and framed those magnificent breasts.

"Yeah, I come here too much."

in the middle of things, 2000

In Medias Res

"What? Why?" The next words I remember saying on the phone.

It was spring and change was in the air. The days were beautiful—getting longer. Everything was coming to life. I saw a snake sunning on a rock this morning.

I wore as much black as possible. I even bought some new tight, black briefs. Really they were too small and my belly lipped over the edge.

"I just quit. It's over. I'm glad."

I couldn't believe it.

"What will you do then? For money? How will you spend your days?"

"I'll get a job in a coffee shop. I'll work in a bakery. I'll sell bicycles. Anything different. Anything with some life in it."

"But your job. Sure, it sucked. Everybody's job sucks. But it was good money. It was structure. It was life."

The line was silent.

"Can you still get it back?"

"No. Why would I want to?"

"I'm coming over."

"Wait."

But the phone was down. I ran to my car and sped to her apartment.

She was waiting on her front porch.

In the sunlight, with the flowers blooming all around her—a simple white dress—she was an angel. An angel of spring, of change. Budding. Natural. Clean. Radiant. Alive.

I got out of my car, lit a cigarette, pushed back my dirty hair and approached.

"Don't you look cheery?"

I looked at myself. Black up and down, inside and out.

I said nothing, just blew a cloud of smoke from the bottom step, below.

———

"It's not that I'm telling you what to do. I don't want that. I'm not that person. But I am questioning. I'm wondering. I'm worrying."

She set her jaw and looked away. Into what? I no longer knew.

"Sure, yeah, you've got to do what you've got to do. Life is change. I understand."

She turned back and focused on me. "Do you? Do you understand?"

My whole body tensed.

Then there was a sparkle in her eye.

"I have an idea." A grin emerged. "I know a place. A place in the mountains. A cabin. We should go. To watch spring come."

I shifted my weight.

"Just the two of us?"

"Yes," she smiled.

I smiled back.

Passing, 2003

A Moment . . . Soon

As she clips the dying heads of the daffodils with regular scissors I find myself losing the acrid taste of my black coffee. Its bite is replaced with sweetness.

She doesn't know me.

I know her in her graceful movements. The delicate dip of her chin as the blossoms drop to the dark earth. The long line of her arm. Her strong calves.

I know how that earth would taste. It's lumpy, chunky and to me, with her there, it would be sweet, like crumbled chocolate cookies.

All I have known is gone now and I am floating peacefully in a void. I know the void is good only because in it I am closer to meeting her. You see this void is only a moment between then and soon. To you a split second. To me, real time. I count my life by these voids.

The black coffee is in the past as is my skin and my nose, even my black shoes. Because, you see, they will all be different when I raise my hand and say hello. The coffee and the shoes are a part of the soon, but they will be different. Because I know, this sounds trite, because of her glow. Her warmth. All will change and I can't wait. But, strangely, in this moment, the delicious tension fulfills me as nothing else can. Except maybe her. This is the dark time between the lights. Without it she would mean less to me and I to her and I to me.

You know how it is. Suddenly things have changed . . . they are different. Your shoes, your finger nails, your coffee are all changed. And you don't know why. But I do. This is what I'm telling you. There is no light without darkness and vice-versa. And in this moment of darkness the light is so much brighter. And when I stand . . . soon . . . and walk over . . . soon . . . and say hello . . . soon . . . this darkness will vanish, overcome by her light, and mine. I will soon glow too, and she may never know why. She will never know that I glow because of this moment in my private, dark, quiet little room.

Ahhh. So here it comes. So long. I must go and this moment must pass. But there will be another. Maybe after I know her she'll do something even more extraordinary than clip the blossoms off dying daffodils.

Bye, sweet moment, goodbye.

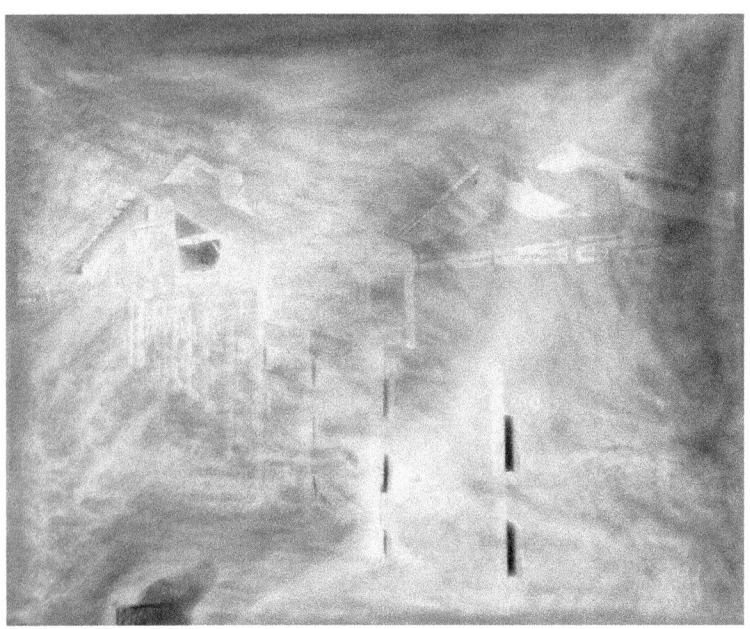

based on actual events, 1997

Part Two

(based on actual events)

Sphinx, 2003

Me, Myself, and I

I am a gay man. By birth, by choice—Does it really matter? I'm here. This is who I am. Deal with me.

I'm not here to explain to you why I am like I am. I'm not here for your forgiveness. I'm just here to tell you about me.

My first experience with a man occurred when I was seventeen—three years after my first experience with a woman— in case you were wondering.

I was working in the local mall—it was the eighties—in a clothing store. I was dating a female co-worker and enjoying it. We had fun. We laughed a lot. We did silly, corny things together like putting on Marilyn Monroe wigs and causing trouble downtown.

Sex for us was really like an extension of our friendship. We were young, inexperienced, wondering what it was all about. We explored each other. We enjoyed it. But it was never like in the movies. It was never that passionate. It was never that romantic, even. It was almost intellectual. "I touch you here, and this happens. Neat!" You know, that kind of thing. All in all, it was innocent, experimental—like playing—not serious.

We also had long, involved conversations about everything— you know, heavy stuff—the future, marriage, what we wanted from life, who we wanted to become—whatever. Everything. Our talks were often more intimate than our sex.

I think that was the one thing she really liked about me— she could talk to me about anything. I, of course, felt the same way. We were very open with each other. Honest. Trusting.

I really just adored her. As a friend. Someone to share secrets with.

One day when this beautiful guy comes into the store, I saw her notice him. She couldn't take her eyes off him. I wasn't jealous. I couldn't take my eyes off him either. He was tall. Blond. Muscles. Very manly. Didn't say much and had this lovely, calm confidence about him. He was young, but still a stud. He bought a leather jacket. Not from me. I had butterflies. I couldn't get near him.

She had walked right up to him. Smiled. Stuck out a provocative hip. And sold him the jacket.

"Nice moves," I said, with a snort after he left.

"What?"

"You selling jackets or . . . something else?"

"Don't be bitchy. It doesn't suit you."

It was weird. She knew. She knew I looked at him. She knew something that I didn't. About me. And I don't think she liked it. Typical.

I didn't think about him sexually. No, not at all. He was just beautiful—like a sculpture.

Do you feel sexually attracted to Michelangelo's David? No. That's what it was like looking at this guy. Like a piece of art. A perfect specimen of manhood.

Later, after work, we went out for coffee. She was hard to pin down. Usually I knew where she was coming from. But not this time. She definitely had something on her mind.

"It's not what you're thinking. I'm not what you're thinking."

She looked up.

"And what are you?"

Voice strained. Veins showing in her neck.

I smiled weakly.

"I'm me, I'm myself. I'm I."

She wasn't convinced.

"All right. He was beautiful—beautiful like a piece of art."

I reached over for her hand. She kept it under the table.

"I love women. I love all beautiful things. I admit that."

Her hand appeared, but was kept at a distance. I took my hand back, stared directly at her, and played my trump.

"I still want to ravage you. I still must have your fingers in my mouth, your beautiful body in my hands, your hot breath in my ear. It's not a big deal. Not nearly as big as my desire for you."

And it worked. Maybe that's what finally made up my mind about women: their vanity. All you have to do is play to their vanity, complement them a little, and you can get what you want—or, rather, not get what you don't want.

Or maybe I was just pissed because she knew something I didn't.

Of course, things like one's sexuality are rarely easy. I think when we try to make them easy, that's when we screw ourselves up.

I remember when I was much younger. I was at a girlfriend's birthday party. All her friends were there. They were my friends too. The group.

Her mother was a wonderful woman. Thoughtful. She had presents for all the kids at the party. She had G.I. Joes for the boys and Barbies for the girls. When she handed them all out, I was last.

Right. Exactly. Just what you're thinking—she only had

Barbies left when she got to me.

"I'm so sorry. I can go get you another one." Her eyes were so sad, so worried. I felt sorry for her.

"No, it's OK. I'll take the Barbie." It felt right. I actually wanted it.

"No, no. I'll get you a man." I remember it so well. Her round face, weak chin, long tapered fingers, dyed hair.

"Could I please have the Barbie?"

She was hesitant and looked around. All of the other kids had gone outside. It was just she and I in their living room.

I really did want it. I had plenty of guy dolls. I wanted a woman.

"Well, OK." She almost smiled.

"Thank you," I said as she handed her over. I wanted her to feel comfortable with it. So when I got the doll, I didn't look at it, I looked at her. I tried to tell her with my eyes that everything would be fine.

And I did feel fine about it. But, I was very aware that I had to make others comfortable. That has been the only consistent truth in my life.

I had to hide my new Barbie from my dad when he came to pick me up from the party. I put her down the front of my pants and pulled my shirt out. He never noticed. But, my father rarely noticed anything. I still don't think he knows I'm gay. Not that I care.

———

I took Barbie home and got her good and married to my eagle-eye G.I. Joe. They were very happy. He carried her to his sturdy jeep and drove her away into a night of steamy sex.

Once he got her undressed, and did his business, he caught himself.

"Barbie, you don't have nipples."

"Oh, Joe, did you really miss them?"

"I wouldn't have if you had pubic hair, but you don't have that either. What the hell kind of woman are you?" Joe spat and pulled up his pants. Then he lifted the hood of the Jeep and checked the engine. But he couldn't think straight. So he paced around, chewing an old cigar butt. Barbie lazed in the back of the jeep—buck naked.

"For God sakes. Cover up. Don't you have any decency?"

"Oh, Joe, there's no one around. And we are married. Come on back over here you big man." She blew a kiss at him and touched herself—down low.

This made Joe even more mad.

"God damn it! Barbie! Stop that! Right now!"

But she wouldn't. She only rubbed harder and faster. And she started laughing.

"Come on you big man! Give it to me Joe! Get over here and treat me like a woman. Treat me like you should!" She screamed—laughing, cackling.

"You witch! You're a demon! You possessed my soul! Damn you! God damn you Barbie!"

And Joe stopped her. Abruptly.

He pulled her by her hair from the jeep and kicked her over the ground. She was laughing, bloody, hurt, cackling. Like a witch.

So Joe took his trusty army-issue scissors and cut her tits off. Yes he did. Clean off. Then he stomped on her face until she shut up. He buried the tits in a special spot, way out behind the house, at night. He could see because of his eagle-eye vision.

Then, as a wedding present, he laid her body in the jeep, fully dressed now. And burned her. And the jeep. The whole kitten caboodle. Then Joe swore an oath to men everywhere and walked away, never to be seen again.

—

Later, when I was a little bit older, I remember playing with my baby-sitter. I would stay at her house. She had a whole collection of dolls.

"Are you sure?"

"Yeah, why not, you want to, I want to. Let's play house."

She looked at me sideways, like her mother used to look at her.

"Come on, it's no big deal."

"Well, all right." Again she imitated her mother, this time with a voice.

And we did. We had fun, but I began to resent her. Why did I have to explain myself? You know—Me—who I am.

And so what? I played with Barbies. Big deal. I'm not worried about it. Why are you?

There was another time, when I was older—ten or eleven.

I loved to dress up.

One year at the beach—the annual family vacation—I took a good friend with me.

Everyone was on the beach except for he and I. We were still in the house.

I was really energetic, excited, hyper, bouncing off the walls. So, I thought I'd play a little joke on him.

He was very masculine for his age. He worked on a farm, had muscles—a man before his time. I liked him. I looked up to him.

Anyway, I went into my mom's room—into her closet—pulled out one of her sun dresses and slipped it on.

It fit me perfectly. It looked good. It felt good.

Then I found a big straw hat and some huge sunglasses and completed the look.

"OK, let's got to the beach!" I pranced out, headed for the door.

He turned and froze. His jaw actually dropped. Then he screamed—really loud.

"What the fucking hell are you god-damned doing!?"

I winked at him and swished to the door.

"Stop! You can't! Stop!" He panicked and charged me. He got me just as I got to the door—grabbed my arm and spun me around—swung at my face.

I ducked and he missed.

That makes me sad, that memory, that event. I know he didn't understand, but, he was my friend. Why couldn't he play along—just for fun?

A few years later I'm losing my virginity to the love of my life. She was my best friend—my lover—everything. I still love her today.

But one afternoon when I came over to her house for a surprise visit, I saw a strange car in the driveway. I thought maybe it was her brother or something. I was just plain stupid—naïve. I walked in.

"Hellooo!"

Then it happened. I saw her naked body dash by the doorway in the other room. I heard a distinct masculine stupid "What?"

My knees gave, I dropped, and my hands slapped the floor.

I dragged myself outside, sobbing, screaming, dying.

And here she comes.

"What the hell are you doing here!?" Just like her. Attack!

Somehow I got into my car and left. That was it.

Through high school I dated some other girls, but it was never the same. I had a lot of fun, but something was never quite right.

Getting a job in a clothing store seemed like a natural enough thing to do. It was in the next town over—away from the people that knew me. And it was better than washing dishes. Commissions. Discounts on clothes. Perfect for a junior in high school. I never even thought what people would think. Other guys I knew were getting construction jobs, working on farms, landscaping. I worked in a clothing store. So what?

Then the rumors started at school. Some of my friends— all girls at that point—told me that people were talking about me. But, I'll tell you, I didn't really care. They wanted to be confused about my sexuality. Fine. I felt no need to explain.

And I met a lot more girls at the mall. Better girls.

Then one day this guy comes into the store. He's older. I'd been working there about six months. The place was not crowded. My co-worker girlfriend and another girl and I were the only people working. And they were both with customers. It was like fate. Like from God fate.

He's not attractive like the statue-boy from before. But he

is persistent.

"Hi. Can I help you?" I put on my usual sales-guy face.

"Well, yeah. Do you ever go to the Dungeon?"

The local gay club.

"No." Butterflies flapping in my stomach. Light-headed.

He came closer. "We should go sometime. It's a great place. Great music. Fun people."

Now, very close.

"Ah . . . " I stammered.

"I know, you're nervous. It's OK. I was too—before. But, you know, my roommate and I got it on a few times in college—and it was fun—freeing. Not scary at all. I just had to let go."

"Ah, um, I . . . "

"It's OK. I'm sorry. I'm so forward. But you're just so cute—so handsome—I couldn't help myself."

Now I know what women have to deal with. Men!

"I, ah, really like girls." My heart was racing. My face was hot.

"It's OK. Do you think dancing with a man will change that?"

"Maybe. Probably."

"It's up to you."

He just looked at me—straight on. I didn't know what to do. My mind and my body and my emotions were scattered in all kinds of directions.

Then he smiled. Warmly. Friendly. And left. Blew away.

He didn't look gay. He didn't act gay. He was no queen. He was just a guy looking for a date.

I found myself watching his butt as he left.

I wasn't afraid of him. Actually, I was flattered. Nobody had ever asked me out before.

Then I looked over and my girlfriend was staring right at me.

She knew what happened.

—

Later, I had coaxed her out to coffee with promises of easy talk and smiles.

"He asked me out."

She took a sip of coffee and brought her eyes very slowly up to meet mine.

"I thought so."

"I said no," I blurted.

"Oh." She exhaled—really she sighed.

"No one's ever done that before. I was kind of flattered."

"Well, sure, I know." She looked away, her smile mechanical.

"You never know what's going to happen," I laughed.

Life had never felt so intense as it did in that moment. I was on the precipice of something new, something real.

She was obviously worried. Maybe I could have done more to ease her fear. But, by that point, I wasn't interested in easing anyone's fears about my behavior. So, I just let it go— whatever we had. Sure, we still talked and were friendly. But the relationship, the sex, the long nights of conversation, were gone forever.

Not two weeks later he came back to the store.

"Hi."

"Hi," he smiled.

He just stood there.

"OK, Friday." I was firm.

"Great." He glowed. Bubbled. Energy. Excitement. A Victory!

"I'll meet you there at ten." Still firm.

I felt the butterflies again and smiled.

Like G.I. Joe, I never looked back.

—

Sex with a man is obviously different from sex with a woman. But, in some ways, it's similar. It's still two people working for mutual pleasure. That's all sex really is anyway.

Love is a different matter altogether. I have to admit, the only person I've loved was a woman. I have greatly admired men. I've been attracted to men. I've had sex with men. I even have respected men. Deeply. Fully. But, I've never loved one.

And yet, I'm gay.

I don't think it's a short-coming. I mean, I've had men say they love me—and do loving things for me—romantic things.

So what is it?, you ask. Why be gay? If it's not about sex—and it is for so many people—what's it about?

It's a slow, confident stride. A firm jaw. Stubbornness. Physical strength. I'm gay because I'm attracted to men. Sure, women are beautiful—worthy of praise—respect—admiration. But they are so . . . feminine.

I'm not feminine.

With a man, it's easy. It's clear. Basic. Whoever is on top is on top. No games.

When I see a beautiful man, I want him. I want him so bad, I want to be in him. I want to be him.

I don't want to be a woman. I don't do drag—except when

I was a kid—and we saw how that turned out.

There's something so sturdy—so reliable—so playful about men. They are the whole package without the baggage. And I learn from them. I learn how to be a man.

You'd be surprised how many seemingly straight guys have had or continually have sexual relations with men. A lot more than you would think.

I like the strong ones. Ones that don't play gay. That look straight. Like a boxer or a Wall Street guy. Yeah, I like men who are in control—who tell me what to do—who tell me how to be more of a man.

Women don't help. They try to make you less of a man. They belittle you, cheat on you, judge you, hurt you, knock you back, yeah, knock you down. With their "encouragement". Their "concern".

So, I'm a gay man. Not for any reason except I like men. I want them. I want to be them. It's perfectly natural for me. I'm fine with who I am. Me, myself, and I.

I just wanted you to know.

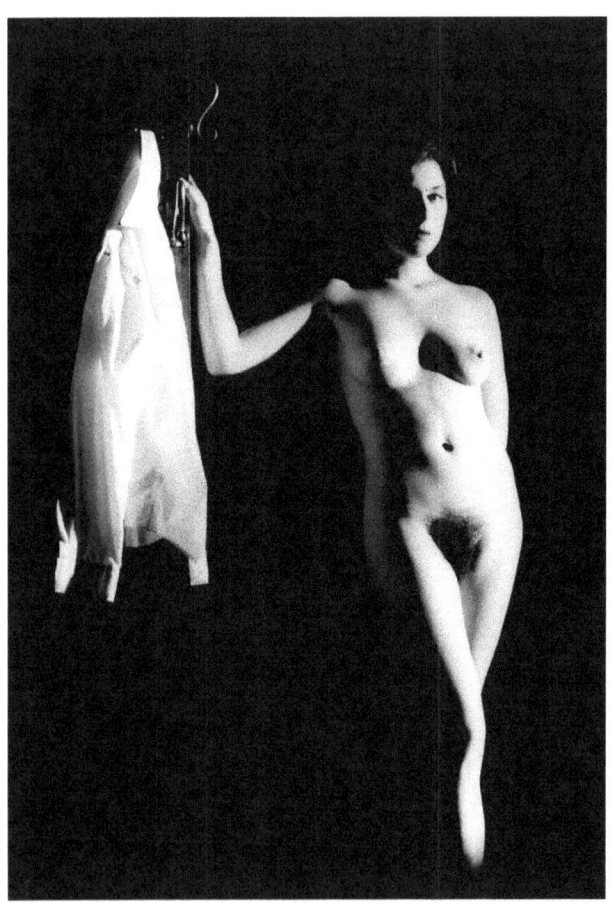

Evin in Blue, 1996

Tied to the Mast

We met at a very strange time in my life. Actually, it was a pretty bad time in my life. I was pretty low, pretty needy. I knew this then. I knew I was weakened.

And when we met at a mutual friend's party I was so taken with her I could barely breathe. There she was, across the room—alone! I couldn't believe it.

She was wearing black boots and long, tight-fitting pants and a cropped sweater—also black. No make-up to speak of and her long, beautifully dark hair just flowed over her shoulders. She was an eye-full for sure. But, she was also so much more. She was rich, a heavy presence. Real. Like a goblet of red wine, or velvet drapes, or an autumnal sunset—dark, but that particular darkness that suggests depth, richness, like mud or chocolate mousse, or the endless expanse of night from atop a high hill in the country, with the wind spreading your hair and gently pushing on your clothes to make them feel just a little bit heavier so you feel the ground under you and the world, the world. That's what she was like. That's what I saw, what I felt, when I first saw her, when my love affair began. I would learn, though, that yes, darkness is richness and that the depths hold many exciting currents of emotion not found on the surface, but I would also find that things are rarely as they seem in the darkness, in the murky depths of a pond, in the darkest hour of night, or at the bottom of the best bottle of red wine imaginable.

I was like a lot of people before I met her. I saw darkness as time for sleep, time given up so that the days could be more productive. And I had never thought of finding richness in life, in things obscure, in things below the surface. I figured that everything I needed was right there in front of me. And if it weren't, I could easily get it, buy it, make it, whatever. I didn't think much about other motivations, motivations unnameable, unmanageable, uncontrollable.

As I said, my life was not so great, and I really didn't know why. Sure, I felt needy. Of course I would get lonely. Yes, I wondered if I would ever meet someone who would affect me deeply, challenge some of my views, open my eyes to something new. But these things became less and less important the longer I lived. So by the time I was at that party I basically had gone numb. But, when I saw her, something—actually many things—rustled around in me, were stirred up, were brought back to life, brought back up.

She was just standing, with a cock to her hip, and a drink lingering near her lips.

And alone. I couldn't believe it. No one was talking to her—and the place was full of people. Why?

She caught my eye and smiled. Her posture changed, became more open, on display. Like she was singing to me. Calling me to her. What could I do? I had to go, or throw up.

So I walked over trying to not be afraid—to not be put-off by her beauty. I was trying to be lively, happy. I felt like she demanded it. I wanted to be happy too, right? Isn't that the point? OK, here he comes, Mr. smiley, happy, fun party guy!

Up close, she was even more beautiful. Her skin, especially around her eyes, was light, making her eyes look very open and interested. I stopped a few feet away, transfixed. She moved closer, into my space, but I didn't back down.

"You look like a painting," I whispered. I really was taken with those eyes, and that neck, and her breath, with her whole, what? . . . musical . . . presence. Unfortunately my entrée was less than perfect.

I knew she knew.

"Thank you. So do you," she said.

"What? A Picasso?"

She giggled. Her eyes never left me. She was interested.

I was drunk immediately. Just spinning and swooning and all of it. Jesus! Could this be happening to me?

Right, right, I know, we were just talking, big deal, so what. But, there was something else. Something strangely atmospheric inbetween us at that moment. The air was more pressurized, hotter, thicker, heavier. Like the eye of a hurricane. Yeah, that's kind of true, I had just spun out of a hurricane in a way. I was on a nowhere track with no energy, no damn motivation.

Was she an angel? An angel in black?

She smiled over her glass. She wasn't waiting though, she was being very active, she was playing her part, she was seducing me. My heart was like disco. Silly, wild, out of control.

She leaned on the door frame and licked the edge of her glass. And that was it. The world was gone. I was in her power. Her dancing eyes, her supple lips, her singing body all had won me. She had won me.

I pulled out a cigarette. She watched. I offered her one. She motioned to the patio, outside. I quickly nodded and out we went.

The air was just getting chilly. Fresh. Invigorating. I already felt different. When I had come into the party I didn't even notice anything about it. Now, it was alive. Buzzing. Electric.

I followed her into the woods near the house, a trail of

smoke from her mouth leading me deeper into the trees.

The leaves under my feet were rustling in rhythm with her. We were truly walking together.

Then we stopped. Never have I ever heard such silence.

And there was the moon, my guardian, my longest lover, floating happily above us, shining through the bare branches.

She caught her breath quickly in her throat. A gasp almost. I think she loved the moon too. Like me. I coughed and pushed my cigarette butt down through the leaves into the damp earth.

She turned. And even though the light of the moon was behind her, I could still see her eyes. Bright. Focused. I wanted to kiss them. I wanted to taste them. I knew they would be fresh, like peppermint.

She moved closer, into my space again. And I just went for it. I pulled her close and brought her mouth to mine. She responded. It was right. She came into me swimming through melodious energy deep, deep into my mouth, my body. And then sensuous rhythm, dancing, flowing, liquid, hot. Rich like chocolate cake. Full in the mouth, succulent.

Our fingers laced behind her back. Her chest was against me and I felt the strong engine of her heart thumping, pulsing with life. I went slack, yet remained upright like a child would when his finger was deep in a live wall outlet. Frozen solid, except thawing on the inside, gooey, sap rising. I was warming. Nothing ever felt more real.

And we came back to earth, having danced with moon, opened our eyes, licked our lips and breathed. The cold couldn't touch us.

She smiled wickedly, took my hand and led me away. Soon we were in my house, under my sheets, and on the floor, the bathroom, the rug, backwards, forwards, left, right. All in unison, all for mutual pleasure, all for good.

I turned the heat off and threw the windows open. Naked, alive, hot flesh, together. She met me in the middle of the room. Her nipples poked into my skin. Her nails ran down my back. My hands combed her hair, pulled it tight. Her breath was hot on my neck and I threw her down to the floor. Then I was in her again. Or she was around me. She was doing more to me than I was to her with her thorough rhythm. Like a beast feeding on me. I just hung on as she pulled me in and out, over and over, until I came so hard I passed out.

I woke up warm under the sheets of my bed. She was watching me, perched on an elbow. The room was freezing.

"How did I get up here?"

"I lifted you." Her voice was honey, sweet, full.

A moment of uncertainty came and then blew away, out the window. I think she only wanted to be there with me. Just like I did.

—

Time passed, but not like before. Days were not endured, rather, they were consumed. Eaten. Swallowed. Enjoyed. She had me. I was hers. Anything and everything for her. All. Delightfully lost in giving, being taken, being used, enjoyed. Everything I ever wanted. Maybe everything she ever wanted too.

—

She loved it when I drove fast. She had no car, and I was

happy to pick her up whenever she wanted it.

At first I did it to impress her—to show how reckless I was. She liked that. After a while though the power had shifted. I may have been at the wheel, but she was driving.

"Do it! Come on!" She laughed and slid the sun roof back—getting ready.

"I'm low on oil."

She was hearing no excuses and ignored me, her eyes directly forward.

Then she inched up her short skirt. She still wasn't looking at me. But she knew I was looking at her. I saw just the tip of her white cotton underwear and my teeth ground.

She slid off her shoes and pushed her strong toes into the floor carpet.

And that was it.

The engine groaned when I down-shifted—so did she, come to think of it. And in seconds we're at a hundred miles an hour.

She's screaming, howling—hands stroking her legs, hair blowing out—the wild song of it all.

Then, in a flash, she reached over and was in my pants. Probing. Pulling.

A hundred and ten. Straight through the abandoned black night.

She's got one hand in my pants and the other in her underwear.

A hundred and twenty.

Now I'm moaning. Now I feel like she does. I *feel* her!

Her eyes are closed, but rolling. She' stroking me, singing, the roar of the wind all around us.

One thirty!

Inside and outside. I yell so hard I hurt my throat.

And BOOM! Black smoke out of the back. No power. The car is dying. I don't care. I yank it out of gear and we coast back down. Slowing. The wind. The roar. She's still stroking me, laughing, her hot hand now squeezing me and she's laughing as we're coasting, the silent road under us ever past. I yell out my window—she yells out her window.

And we pulled into somebody's driveway and groped and kissed and pounded into each other on the burning-hot hood of my car. Bam! Over.

———

See, you have to understand. In so many ways she was independent, mature—unique—but she was young. She was still innocent of her power. She knew how to push the buttons, she knew how to get what she wanted. But she didn't know why. It was more than just her beauty. At the time she didn't know though. She thought that's all she was. And she was wrong.

———

Once, we're at this party and it's like she's holding court. The whole group is sitting around her—sitting on the floor— and she's on the edge of the couch in a tight sweater.

She spoke, she listened, she laughed, she argued, she charmed, and generally kept everyone rapt with her song. Everyone but me.

I was in another room. Her magic spell was not on me this night. I knew because I could feel the energy pouring from the other room, blowing into my small, cold corner of the party.

At some point, she did come to check on me.

"Having fun," I asked.

"Yes. Absolutely." She saw me. Saw through me. "You should come and join us."

I laughed.

She flashed me the innocent eyes and unconsciously smoothed a non-existent wrinkle.

"Unless you don't want to."

"I'm fine here." I wasn't giving anything. "I was watching the fire."

"Is anything wrong? Are you sad?"

"No, not at all. Contemplative. Enjoying the quiet."

She crossed her arms behind her back. Her breasts came forward. I know she did it to show me how desirable she was. But, her chin dropped and she cast her eyes down and sighed.

"I'm having fun in there. I wish you'd come with me."

"I'll be here when you're done. You don't need me to have fun. Not tonight."

She straightened her spine and brushed a stray hair into place.

"It is all right you know." She gave me a sympathetic grin, turned, fixed her sweater, and went back to the spotlight.

My guts turned to pudding and dribbled down into my legs. My head was light. I had to escape.

I struggled to the kitchen, grabbed the first bottle I saw, checked my jacket for cigarettes, and went out into the cold.

———

By the time we were driving home I couldn't see straight. She was next to me, but unavailable. Beautiful like the moon, and as far away.

She didn't notice the speed, or the red lights I ran, or the car I almost side-swiped—or even the bum I almost hit.

Or maybe she did. And she liked it. She liked my recklessness—my self destruction. By not stopping me, she was encouraging it. I realized that's what she wanted all along.

The timing was perfect. I floored it into the turn coming off the interstate. I looked over at her and somehow, she seemed sad. I was confused and never saw the ice.

Suddenly, we're sliding sideways and the world is in a blender—but all black. The back end of my car came swinging around the front. I just let go of the wheel—dropped my hands into my lap—left it up to God. She cackled as we hit the gravel, skidded and then stopped, pointed the wrong way in the grass by the off-ramp.

I looked at her, the engine still running.

"Are you all right?"

She was cackling, laughing low in her throat. I thought she was choking.

"Oh my god! Are you all right!?"

She turned to me and I saw a face unfamiliar—a visage of aggression—malignancy and joy—mouth wide open—nostrils flared—eyes hungry—and the whole thing on fire.

"Again!" Her voice like a man's, heavy with lust.

I hesitated.

"NOW!"

I was terrified and instantly sober.

"Do it! God damn it! Do it!"

So I did. I spun out of the grass, up the off-ramp, back up the highway, circled back and approached the ramp for a second time. The whole time she was stone—smooth, chilling.

I eased into the turn and punched it again. The ice threw us sideways out of the road, through the gravel, around in a circle and back into the grass.

Belly laughs. Hoots, screams, cackles. Fingernails in my thigh.

And she was on me. Hands searching—hungry.

"Again. More!" Her hot breath enveloped me, intoxicated me. Her elbows were dancing. Her eyes all over. Her breath short. Her breasts in my throat.

"Now! More! Now!" She had me in her hands. I was iron-hard. So hard it ached. She's pulling me to her.

And I realized right then that what she wanted was what I wasn't. She wanted unmetered, reckless abandon—wildly, madly, fully, surging through her veins—and fucking me—and fucking with me—was as close a she could get.

"No," I whispered. "No."

She tightened her grip to let me know she could hurt me.

"Yes," she hissed.

"No. I'm sorry. No."

"Fuck you!" She squeezed me hard then pushed back over to her seat, leaving me cold, exposed.

"Take me home," she spat. Arms crossed.

I just stared into the darkness for a long minute.

"Now God damn it! Now!"

"It seems your vocabulary is shrinking," I said as I tucked myself back into my pants and zipped up. Then I put my car in gear and slowly motored back onto the off ramp and away.

———

She wanted my destruction. And she wanted to watch.

What now?

Time passes. Passions become malignant. Togetherness decreases to long, boring phone calls.

"Oh come on, don't be this way! He's a friend. I've known him for a long time."

"That much is clear."

She was silent.

"I understand that we both need a little space. I understand that you're not happy with me now. I understand where you're really coming from," I said.

We were both silent, though my breathing was heavy.

"No, you don't"

"What?"

"You don't understand where I'm really coming from. No, not at all." Her voice was calm, measured, unreadable.

"What?"

"I don't need your permission."

"For what?" She was losing me. On purpose I think.

"I don't need this! You don't trust me!"

"Why should I?" It just slipped out. I regretted it immediately.

I heard the phone smack the wall on her side.

Instantly I saw myself as that phone, in her apartment, a tiny little nothing in the palm of her hand and then slammed against the hard wall. I felt it. Oh, yes she got the reaction she wanted.

And I waited, and waited.

Then she was screaming at the phone—at me.

"God damn it! God damn it! What is your fucking problem?! I just want something different—just to see a friend.

It's not bad, it's not wrong! I haven't DONE anything! I won't do anything!"

"You better not," I whispered.

Then I heard her big, heavy shoes stomping around on her wooden floors. The distance between us was all too real.

Then she kicked the phone, I guess. CLOMP, CLOMP, CLOMP, WHAM! And I went spinning across the room. My chest vibrated. My knees chattered. I was glad to be sitting. I was smashed on the rocks.

And I hung up.

That's it.

'sposed to be a tiger, 1999

A Mouth Full of Marbles

"I think that we should not see each other any longer." She paused in disbelief of her statement. "It's not that I don't like you. And I certainly want to be your friend, you know, still see each other as friends, but I can't seem to manage the physical and the emotional side of our relationship." She pursed her lips and squinted at him.

He looked at her. "As always, you are right on the mark. I feel the same way. My emotions are so screwed up that I don't even know what I believe in any longer. I just wanted things to work. There were too many reasons for us not to be together, and I guess that I wanted to beat those odds." He paused, looking confused. "That's not what I wanted to say or even how I wanted to say it. Sorry."

She smiled for the first time, and looked on him as a child. "It's all right. I'm very confused myself. We have had some great experiences together, and I'm sure that we can have more, just not as a couple." She looked to him for agreement. "It's really weird, I feel like we could spend our lives together and have gorgeous babies, and be happy, but I also feel that I've lost myself in trying so hard to make things work between us. I find myself not even knowing what I want when I'm alone."

"Me too. When we're not together, I look for you in your things at my house. I look for the answers to my questions in your hairbrush. It's very strange." He looked down.

She continued his thought. "It's because we are so different. We give each other a perspective that each of us hasn't found anywhere else. And I think that on an intellectual level that is very appealing, but as we are both still trying to find ourselves, we argue and take things out on one another to sort of stake our claims, to push off each other to establish our own identities." She broke, and then continued. "And by trying to follow the norm and make a relationship out of our being together, we only confuse ourselves and hurt each other. And I don't want to hurt you. I love you and I respect you, but I guess that I don't respect myself enough to acquiesce to your needs." The waitress interrupted them with fresh coffee and they both relaxed, glad that neither had to vocalize the need to stop the conversation.

For a long while they both sat and thought, looking at each other, sometimes smiling, sometimes seeming perplexed, but always thinking of the other in relation to themselves. Their passion was so great individually, and when together, they both flip-flopped across the fence of their decision many times. She was exceptionally sad for most of the silence as she felt little direction now that he was leaving her life. She was disappointed in herself for sacrificing so much of her time for something that didn't look as though it was going to pan out in her favor. She continued to question herself.

He listened to his thoughts as they streamed through his head. They said many things to him. One being: "Run away, save yourself and get the hell out of there." Others said to him that he must trust and respect her. He did care for her, right? He should pass over his own need for her in his life and do whatever he could to help her. One last stray thought flashed angrily in his head: "What a fucking bitch!" How could she do this to him after all that he had done for her? All of the good times that they had were worthless and why the fuck should he do anything for her when she could just walk away from him, and all that he had given her?

She looked up and noticed he was scowling. "I have had so much fun with you. You have treated me better than any other boyfriend that I have had and I want you to know that."

He was still angry.

"Well if that isn't the most pleasant send off I've ever heard." He slugged back his coffee, forgetting that he had put neither sugar, nor cream in it. The acrid taste soothed his mind somehow. He wasn't shocked or threatened by it. Rather, he was brought back to himself. For a moment he was clear. Then he looked into her eyes and he grew more confused.

She dispassionately flicked her ash from her cigarette, then she looked at his blank face hoping for a way back into the conversation and him. She got nothing and was miffed at his usual moody isolation. She tried him anyway. "Where are you?" Lowering her eyes to her empty plate she hoped he would not raise his voice.

"I'm here. I'm just confused as usual. What I don't understand is why we can't, you know, make it work, somehow." She looked up to him, smiling.

"We've had that discussion so many times and it never seems to get us anywhere, and I don't think that having it now will help either one of us." She was pleased that she could speak coherently about something that she had learned through her emotions.

He only sighed.

"It's amazing how far the human race has come. I mean, we're still fucked up, but we have made great lengths in understanding the physical world. It's the emotional that still confuses us. People like us have had this same conversation and these same problems for centuries, and I'm sure that they have solved them in many ways, but this convergence, the agreement of two people who are so different really only works in fiction, doesn't it? I mean, in movies, and books, people come against great odds and then they get together. In sonnets and poems, people work things out. But in real life, this here, now, it seems so foreign, unattainable."

"Maybe ours is not an isolated case. Maybe all people that try to get together want it to be like it is in the movies."

"The fiction of it is the ease. I think people do get together and surmount great odds all of the time, but it is not easy, for anyone."

They both nodded to themselves and felt a little better.

Thicket, 1999

Between the Lies

"I feel like my whole life has been a downward spiral," he said as he pulled a match from the book and struck it with a flick of his wrist.

"That sounds pretty depressing," she said. Her wine glass was half empty and the lipstick smudge on the rim caught the light of the candle, distorting it.

—

They had met one another in the grocery store a few months ago. He was searching through the fresh vegetables to find some tomatoes.

She was quickly pushing her cart through the beer section, looking for her favorite import.

He was collecting the contents for a homemade marinara sauce that he was going to make for his friends that night. The three of them were celebrating the opening of their new bar.

As he picked through the tomatoes, he was mentally running through the rest of his shopping list. Since he was in a hurry, he paid little attention to what he was doing, mindlessly putting them in a plastic bag and then dropping them into his basket.

"OK I need some spices for the sauce. They are on the other side of the store," he thought to himself as he pushed the basket forward.

Having found her beer of choice, she carefully marked it off of her shopping list. She looked up through drooped glasses and caught his eyes as he approached.

The blacks of his pupils looked like bullet holes in the middle of a blue sky.

They were held, locked together for that moment as their baskets moved directly at one another.

Then she looked down and swerved out of his way. As she moved along, he slowed and turned, watching her go. She didn't notice that this happened. She was stunned from his direct stare.

As her image faded in his mind, he noticed the stack of beer bottles in his path. He closed his mouth and the urgency of his situation came back to him.

"Spices. I've got to get spices and get out of here," he thought as he glanced down at his watch. He was running late.

When he reached the spice rack, she and her glasses had magically appeared at the pasta section which was directly opposite on the aisle.

She didn't notice him. She was looking at her list.

He noticed her. Spices left his mind like pigeons from a coop. He was frozen and staring.

She was noticeably shorter than he, even though her shoes had small heels. Her waist-length black wool coat was deceiving. It made her look heavier than she was. But she had thin legs. He was not dissuaded. He liked the way her dark, shoulder-length hair covered the collar of her coat.

Suddenly he felt something in his gut. Its slippery motion reminded him most of warm fudge sauce slithering into his stomach. It sickened him a little as it began to flicker as if the sauce had glass mixed in with it. A tiny burst of air escaped his flaccid lips.

His feet began to move. Inside he was screaming at his feet to stop their forward motion, but they would not. The flickering of the fudge began to feel more like molten lava as he drew closer to the pasta side of the aisle. His mind raced through images of planes crashing and nuclear explosions as another volcanic shot of air escaped his lips. His eyes went wide and his breath grew heavy in his throat.

"Excuse me."

She turned the other way, unaware of where the noise came from. He coughed. She looked around at him.

"I was wondering if you could suggest a pasta to me. I'm making a dinner for some friends," he said as he wiped his moist brow.

When she recognized him, her eyes widened slightly and she tightened her grip on her shopping list.

"Oh. Well, what are you making?" She regained herself and turned to face him.

"I have this old family recipe for marinara sauce and I need some pasta to go with it. I always find pasta so confusing. There are so many kinds you know," he smiled. His legs felt like pillars of granite.

"Angel hair might be good. It cooks really fast too." She said through her widening smile.

He smiled back and swallowed deeply. He followed her eyes to the wall of pasta in front of them.

She pulled down a package of the angel hair and handed it to him.

"This is the kind I always use. It's good." His hand met hers on the package. Their thumbs were separated by the label on the top while their fingers just touched underneath.

A breath of her perfume tickled his nose and he quickly

brought the pasta toward him, then rested it on the edge of his cart so she wouldn't see his hands tremble. His stone legs began to quiver at the knees.

"Thanks. This looks great." He said forcing himself to remain erect.

"Um, ah, would you mind if I were forward with you?" he said.

"Well, it depends how forward you are." She was impressed. That she couldn't hide. He knew it.

Though shaken, she kept her eyes on his. Her fingers nervously began twisting the list in her hands.

"Would you like to come to this party tonight? Well, it's not really a party. Two of my friends and I are celebrating tonight." He smiled.

"What are you celebrating?" She noticed her fingers twisting the list and moved them to behind her back.

"We just opened a bar together. We're business partners. They're bringing the beer and I'm making the food." He straightened his back and felt a twinge of pain in his shoulders.

"What time?" Her words escaped her mouth out of her control. She tensed her grip on her fingers behind her back.

He gripped the package of pasta tighter and said eight o'clock. The flicking lava light in his gut clicked onto its full brightness as he held down another burp.

"I think that would be fine. Can you pick me up?"

He smiled and thought: "I just did."

—

The aroma of the restaurant was that of New Orleans in the summer time. Its thick, hot smell lingered with them as they looked down at their empty plates.

He lit another cigarette as he watched her thumb slowly move across her glass, smearing her lipstick.

"We met in the grocery store right?" He was struggling to find something to talk about.

"You know very well that we did. You were looking for pasta and I wasn't looking for anything." She glared at him. It was dim in the restaurant and she could barely make out the blues of his eyes.

"Did you talk to me or did I talk to you?" He watched the smoke trail away from the burning tip of his cigarette.

"We talked to each other. You asked me about pasta and then asked me out." Her voice was tense.

"Oh, that's right. I was celebrating the opening of my bar. That was a good night." His eyes drifted from hers to the waitress across the room as he searched for something to say. "You have a great figure you know."

"Thanks. Must be why I'm so good in bed."
His head whipped around. Her dark eyes reflected the candle light.

"What's the matter with you?" he asked.

"What did I have for dinner?" she asked and then drained her wine glass.

"What?"

"You heard me. Or did you?" She reached for the pack of cigarettes and the matches.

"You had chicken." His brow drew close to his eyelashes.

"What wine did I have with my dinner?" she asked as she dragged the match across the book. The tiny flame burst between them and she slowly brought it to the tip of her cigarette.

He looked to her glass and said, "Red." His eyes glanced up

and caught hers through a cloud of smoke over the table.

"When's my birthday?" she asked.

"Hey, why all of the questions? What is this? An interrogation?" He pushed back into his chair and looked away.

"We should go." The corners of her mouth drew into a tight grimace and she sighed through her nose.

"What? Why? We haven't had dessert yet." He looked back, glaring, confused, searching. Now she looked away. He leaned back into his chair and took a long drag from his cigarette.

They both exhaled and were surrounded by the din of the restaurant. The distant sounds of activity in the kitchen mingled with the hum in the low light of the people at other tables talking around them.

"I don't like dessert. I've got to get up early anyway." She snubbed out her half-smoked cigarette and stood up. "Will you get the check while I go to the bathroom?" She wedged her purse under her left arm and stared down at him. Her elbow pushed the purse into a dent, her eyes right down at him.

"Well, sure. Go ahead." He paused. His neck muscles tensed as he noticed her purse under her arm. "Yeah, go ahead. I'll get the bill." He flipped his head back at her motioning her to hurry along.

She turned and walked away.

As she receded into the darkness, he glanced across the room for the waitress, and wondered how he could get her number before she got back.

No Outlet, 1999, 2014

Lapses

Madness can be explained, to a point. Then it makes up its own rules. It defies all logic we subscribe to it and can only be truly understood by one immersed in it. To attempt to help one considered mad we must first ask: Do they wish to be healed?

Dr. M. Lees,
attending.

When I had my first breakdown, at the age of twenty, they said it was just stress and a little dehydration.

They said to slow down, relax—try to enjoy my life more. Find joy in simple things. The usual.

They said for me to take a look at my childhood—to look for clues in my past that might show me where my insane work ethic came from. They wanted me to find the things that my parents did and made me do and what things I made myself do when I was younger.

They asked me why did I think I worried so much.

I don't know.

Do you think you worry? The man with the beard asked.

Well, yeah. About the things that matter. Important things.

Such as? The woman at the end of the table asked.

Money.

They weren't as stunned as I hoped. They were silent. Their eyes were tugging at me for more. Our first stand off.

I was calm. I had given them a perfectly reasonable and true answer. They were going to have to work for any of the good stuff. They made so much money. They were so smart. Why not earn a little the hard way?

Your parents are still living?

Yeah.

Simple enough. Though you've got to watch these people. Nothing is simple with them. No, nothing at all.

Where?

On a farm. In Virginia.

Did you work for them? As a kid, a young man?

Yes, to both.

Why'd you leave?

I came to the city to seek my fortune.

Any siblings?

A sister.

What does she do?

Sells her flesh.

Aha! I got them good. All ten eyes popped wide—even if just for a moment.

I see. Does she live here? In the city?

Yeah.

Do you see her?

Occasionally.

They must have seen something in my eyes. They shuffled papers and coughed and generally realigned themselves for another attack. That I knew. I was watching them closer than they were watching me.

Do you disapprove of her? Of what she does?

Yeah. Yeah, I do.

Is that why you shot her?

It was my turn for the eyes bugging out.

What!?

They didn't budge. All the time their eyes were boring into me like diamond bits.

I saw her yesterday. She was fine. A tramp, but fine. And now you're telling me she's shot. Dead?

Not dead. Very lucky.

I leaned back. So, what's the big deal?

Nothing. Stone wall on the other side of the table. Bastards. Whatever.

Maybe they were lying to see how I'd react. So, I gave them the stone face back. Arms crossed. Hatches battened. Fuck you.

You little guinea bugs. Look at you! I had to laugh. They were really stunned now.

Then all was quiet—for how long I don't know.

. . . a wing in air . . .

I see her irregularly. There are some I see—too many—regularly. But, she, she just appears, unannounced, unplanned—out of nowhere. Like when you're walking down the street and the air's kind of cold and the sun is obscured by thick clouds and it's not really cold—just kind of cold—comfortably cold. And it's certainly not warm either and all of a sudden this frisky draft

passes you—runs through your hair—touches your earlobes—
and then goes away. Bracing.

She's like that.

Completely unexpected and so wonderful and quick so that only
by the time she's gone do you realize she was there. In the
moment, you don't actually have time to react. She moves like
the breeze. Faster than thought. So you only have a memory—
an impression—of her. And a little tickling sensation. On your
earlobes.

That's how it was yesterday—and the day before that—and,
maybe today, it will be the same again. We've never met.
Though she has touched me. And, she has noticed me too. We
have met each other's eyes in here. But, that was months ago.
And yesterday. Maybe today.

I suspect that maybe if I spent two hundred hours with her, I'd
probably have the same feeling though—that she was a breeze,
a wing in air. Moving out in the world. Living. And my time
would not be marked by being with her, but by being without
her—with only a feeling, an impression. And, just like now,
when I don't know her, I'd be wanting more—always more.

And, if I did know her, I'd be putting this demand on her—
mostly consciously, but, really, mostly unconsciously—and she'd
hate me for it. Yet she'd like me enough to ask what I want.
And I could only respond honestly.

I don't know. I want you. But, I say this to myself because I know she'd get angry if I said it out loud.

And, then, now, here she is. The breeze sweeps in the open door. No one around in here really notices—people come in and out all of the time. But, I was thinking about her. I was waiting for her. And, amazingly, here she is. Now passing beside me through the space and now at the counter. Her long coat flat to me as I look at her back up there at the counter.

And she moves, the hem sweeping, to cream and sugar. And, if you will, some others leave the table there by the window, near the door, just perfect timing, as she turns that way.

And, now, she's sitting there, by the window. And her lips go tight, her hands around her cup on the table. And, she turns to look at me.

I sit back and fold my hands in my lap, our eyes connected.

Like a cat, like a caged animal, she couldn't hold my stare, and looked away. And it was a beautiful gesture. Just her eyes— her deep, Caribbean eyes—sun high penetrating wild, moving blue—just slid away—like a cat slips away—into the shaft of sunlight hitting the wooden threshold of the doorway.

Still, I stared. But, I tried very hard to relax. I could feel my brow rise and the wrinkles around my eyes recede. My shoulders dropped.

She shifted. One leg of the chair scraped the linoleum—not evenly or smoothly—but jaggedly. Forced.

Then she looked back at me. As an insult she folded her hands in her lap too.

This thrilled me. Gave me a tickle in my belly. She had always been so passive. But this was something new. Gusto. Abondonza.

I must have smiled—no—I know I did. Just a crack, but a smile. Lightening of the eyes. Shoulders easy.

Then I slowly laid my hands flat, palms up, on the cool tabletop, open to her.

She looked away and then just a quick move—her index finger slid purposefully behind her ear pushing that gorgeous dark hair of hers.

Then she focused those Caribbean eyes on me again. And there it was: the twinkle. Small, but there.

And, for the first time, I breathed. I didn't even know I wasn't. The air came to me, came into me, pushed at me, fluttered right up my nose, down my windpipe with force, and down into my chest, filling it.

. . . and the world goes white . . .

Why did you do that? The one with the beard asked.
  What?
  You mean you don't know?
  What? I was sitting here.

No, no you were not.

Could I have some aspirin? My head hurts. I stared.

Of course, they never brought me any.

Then they were all chattering away with concealed voices. I couldn't hear them. They were all very animated. Then the woman at the end of the table broke from the group and looked at me.

You told us a story about a woman in a shop with Caribbean eyes and moving like the wind—like a wing in air, I think you called her. But, you spoke with a British accent—her gawking eyes—which was very convincing, I might add.

She looked over at the others—eyes now beady. Then back at me—accusing.

Would you say your sister had Caribbean eyes?

I sputtered my lips at them but something flashed. I knew they were out to get me, but there was still something. Were they right? Of course not!

Ha! No I did not! You're just scared! You're making it up—just to throw me off! I tried to stand up but noticed that I was bound to the chair.

You just want to keep me here! Tied up. Not free. Trapped! A knowing glare from all.

It hurt. Inside and out, it hurt me to be there in front of them. In front of you Dr. Lees.

So what if I shot my sister? I didn't. She's trash. To be

disposed of. Maybe recycled. Maybe.

You asked me if I worry. Yes I do. But not about money. I worry about freedom. Nobody really has it. We're all tied together in this sick, twisted web. Everything is related. Everyone is related. Don't you see that if I hurt her, it hurts me. And if you hurt me, it hurts you? Don't you see?

Some see competition. I see community.

You want me to tell you what to think about me and I just can't do it. I can try and I can try some more, but, really, are you going to understand? Is that the point? For you to understand me? Are you going to get the right information so you then can have a tidy little concept—an IDEA—of how to assess me—how to look at me—how to think about me? Will that make a difference? To me? I really don't think so. So, what can I do for you today? What if it's completely different from yesterday? Does that mean something? Will you keep trying too? For what? For who? I mean, really, what is identity? Who am I anyway? Who are you? What are you?

You little guinea bugs with your wily ways and your questions.

Graffiti, 1994

Checkmate

The sun had fallen behind the vacant apartment buildings across the street. The street was growing dark. The alley cats were crawling from their hiding places to start their evening prowl for food. I plopped into the wicker chair on my porch, pulled my robe over my knees, and lit a cigarette. I was the king of all I surveyed.

The smoke drifted lazily from my mouth out into the cool evening air as I watched the cats. The usual four were perched in their positions one house away from each other. They acknowledged me the way they acknowledged each other—with indifference. I accept full responsibility for my situation.

Licking and wiping themselves, they prettied their few good spots. One of them looked as though he had seen some rough action since I'd seen him the day before. His tawny fur was matted to his left side with the remains of some escaped blood. He seemed not to mind it as he rubbed his head with his right paw. The other three were as equally battered. Their ears were torn, their tails were bent and crooked. They looked like a terrible bunch of soldiers, pawns in a larger game. I guess I could take care of them, feed them, but I'm not good at that.

Cats are territorial and independent. Maybe that's why I like them.

I flicked my smoldering butt out to the road. Six pairs of eyes and one stray one watched the trailing cinder as it hit the road. One of the cats was missing an eye. I lit another cigarette.

As I breathed in the heavy smoke I thought about my house.

My situation.

My roommates had moved out a month ago leaving me a six month lease on a three bedroom house. Jerks. Thought they were better than me.

He was just getting started at some brokerage firm or something. She rode show horses for very rich people. They were a great couple—very well matched. I was dead weight.

"It's not that we don't like you. It's just that our lives are different," she said one day in the kitchen. The place was a mess. I know, I should be more considerate, but, damn it, I live here too.

She looked down at me. She was tall and with the heels that she so loved to wear—she was immense, imposing, frightening. And a damn snob.

"You think I'm lazy don't you?" I said from below.

She produced a little laugh, covered her mouth and everything. Who the hell did she think she was? Royalty?

"No, it's not that. I just think that there need to be some ground rules if this cohabitation is going to work."

"Like what?"

"Like each of us cleaning up after ourselves."

I wasn't backing down. Who was she to push me around?

"All right. Then I have a ground rule of my own."

I watched her. She swished her nose unconsciously, like any suggestion from me was unsavory.

"Yes, I'm waiting."

"Noise. Keep down the noise."

She put a hand to her chest and took a quick breath.

"Whatever could you mean?"

"I think you know. It's not the front door slamming. It's something else slamming." Tactless, but effective. She gasped for real now.

"Are you suggesting?"

I smiled. She knew exactly what I was suggesting.

"How dare you!" She went rigid. "You listen to . . . us?" Her face went red.

"Believe me, if had a choice, I wouldn't. With the whoops and aaaaahhhhs and moans and rhythmic thumping, I really can't ignore it. At least it doesn't last very long."

"My god, you are an animal! You despicable man!" She choked. "No, this certainly will not work. No it will not!" And she stepped around me and shook her prissy little ass right out of the kitchen.

I felt good. Warm inside. I stood up for myself.

—

When he returned that night he knew something was up. He knew things weren't right. He could feel it, I guess.

"Hi," I said from the couch.

"Hey. Where is she?"

"Crying, I think."

His face sank and he dropped his briefcase. "Whatever for?"

"You ask her," I said as I turned up the volume and ignored him.

He dashed out of the room and upstairs.

I turned the volume back down. I could hear them moving and arguing—strained, almost quiet, voices from above.

She was moaning and crying and in general hysterics. Which was good. Someone needed to rock her little boat.

He was trying to be calm—and to calm her. I heard a

surprised "What" every now and then—and even a "I can't believe it".

I was proud of myself. This place was one third mine and they had to accept that.

The strange thing was, I liked them. They could be very funny and they always invited me along when they went out.

And when I met my girlfriend, we double-dated for a while. They really were nice people, but they were nice to get things, not for any other reason. At least that's how I saw it then.

Soon he came stomping down the stairs. He spun around the corner and flicked off the T.V.

"Why in the hell did you say those things to her?"

I played dumb, because I knew I had spoken the truth.

"You can not treat people like that—especially your friends."

I raised my eyebrows. He noticed.

"What? Are we not friends?"

"You tell me." I sat up.

"I didn't think that was in question. Things have been fine so far."

"For you."

"What's that mean?"

"It means I'm sick of trying to fall asleep to your fucking. At first I thought it was funny, now I don't."

"How? What? I can't believe you!"

"Ah, but you must, for it is true."

He pumped up his chest, a biological reaction I'm sure. He felt threatened. I was getting to him.

"Well, then you should start looking for another place." He was trying to be confident.

"You're forgetting something. It's my place. I signed the lease."

His mouth twisted and he scrunched his brow—like a prune. Mr. Sour Face.

"This is the type of thinking that has pissed me off. You all think it's your place and that if you give me a few pats on the head every now and then, you can do what you want."

"Do you really believe that?" He was pacing.

"More and more all the time."

"Well, if you had a real job, maybe you'd get more respect from us." There it was. Now he was showing his true colors.

"Ah ha! Let the truth be told. You are jealous of my free lifestyle."

"Hardly," he spat.

"Why else would you be so bothered?"

"Because you're an asshole!"

And that was it. They were gone within a week. You've got to fight for what's yours in this life.

So I picked up a second job. The all-night convenience store up my street needed a night clerk.

I doubt I'll ever see them again. Fine with me.

—

One of my neighbors across the street has disappeared from his stoop. I see his crooked tail limp down the alley next to his house. The colors of the other three are hard to make out in the fading light. I forget which of them is the grey one and which is the dirty white one. The black cat looks like a shadow with one glowing yellow eye as he sits and stares at the empty bush next to his house. His tail flicks with interest as the slight wind scatters up the fallen leaves.

—

When they first moved out, my girlfriend would come over a lot. Just the two of us in that big house. We watched movies, played hide-and-seek, chess. It was great.

Once she came over to my house after she got off work. She was acting weird. She didn't say anything. Then she closes all of the shades and turns on the stereo. A great, slow, sexy song began and she moved me to the couch. I fell back comfortably and watched. Her eyes were directly on me as she stepped into the middle of the room.

I never much liked the song until that night. She smiled devilishly down at me and started moving—flowing—like water—like a snake—like Martha Graham.

She started with her shoes—flicked open the laces, and kicked them away. Then her stockings—peeled off those strong legs—fell empty on the floor. And drums behind her—around her.

She slid her hands up her long legs to reach the buttons in the back of her skirt.

The melody—syncopated, rhythmic, dirty.

She ran her hands down her thighs, over her knees. She had gorgeous knees.

Then her skirt dropped to floor right in time with the explosion of trumpets.

She deftly stepped out of it and then placed her hands on her hips, stretching her back and throwing her mess of dark hair behind her.

I couldn't move a muscle—but my heart raced.

The song was booming throughout the empty house when she got to her blouse. Its slow, sultry beat was throbbing under a thunderstorm of guitars, trumpets, saxophones.

She used her left hand to unbutton her blouse while her right brushed back her hair. Once the buttons were free she arched her shoulders backward, let her sinuous arms flow behind her and the blouse dropped to the floor on top of the empty skirt.

She looked like a summer wind that blows life into magnolia blossoms. The queen of life. Unafraid of being exposed—empowered by it.

The music fell away and she shook her hair over her mischievous smile. Waiting.

The air was thick—gravy—melted chocolate.

Then it started quietly behind her. She moved her hands up her sides, down the small of her back, into her white cotton underwear. And she leaned over, sliding them to the floor, bending, revealing the full line of her long legs.

As the music gained momentum for its finale she raised up with her arms at her sides and turned to face me. And just as the music flourished, she unhooked her bra from the front and threw her arms straight above her. The bra flew away and there she was—naked—perfect—heaving with strength, and lust in the center of my silent house.

Magical. To be revered.

Then she jumped to the couch and attacked me.

—

I don't listen to that song anymore. Soon after I got my second job our relationship began to wane. It was almost impossible for us to be together because she had to be at work early in the mornings, usually the same time that I would be getting off. We don't see each other.

She said I never saw her as a person—that I saw her as an object.

Maybe so.

—

Now the sun has completely disappeared. So have the cats. My head is spinning from too many cigarettes and I have to get ready for work.

I stand and salute the cats, where ever they are, and pick up my cigarettes. Before entering the house I throw my arms behind me and stretch my back. I accept my life. I've made some mistakes. So what? Who cares?

The cool air around me feels moist as if it might have some rain in it soon. I guess I'll have to take my coat to work tonight.

Fixed, 1997

we all fall down

It was perfect. Well, close to perfect. As close as anything in my life has ever been to perfect. Well, sure, it had its problems, but they were manageable. What are problems anyway? Challenges, that's what they are. And challenges are good. They give you something to push against. They give you a reason to grow. Unfortunately, we rarely grow spontaneously—like plants. We don't grow like plants. They do a better job. Because they do it spontaneously. They don't think about it. They just do it. We have to think about it. Talk about it. We're not like plants very much. It's too bad. In a way.

Whatever.

It was perfect though. Her car was broken and I was in the business of fixing cars at that time.

It was one of those days when it's cold and wet. And the sky can't make up its mind whether to rain or snow. So it does both. I remember exactly the time because I had just gotten back from a break. At that job, I liked my breaks. I wanted the job because I liked working on cars. I still like cars, I don't have the job anymore though.

I got fired.

They hired me as a mechanic, but they were short in

customer service. So, I got to work in customer service with the ongoing premise that I would be in the shop. Very soon.

Well, it never happened and that's why I got fired. Because I told them, after six months, that I wanted to be a mechanic. They told me I was doing so well in customer service. I told them I wanted to work on cars, not work with people. I like cars. Less trouble. They said, "a few more months" and I could be a trainee. I said go to hell. They said, no, you first. That was about it. I've had a lot of jobs.

But, that job brought me to her. Or, it brought her to me. It brought us together. For that, I am happy. And I am rarely happy.

So, it was a rainy, snowy, cold damn day. I had just gotten back from my break. And she walked in. For once, I wanted to be in customer service.

She came right up to my desk.

"Hi. I called earlier and they told me to just come in. Just to bring my car in."

Her voice wasn't a song. It was a breeze moving lightly through the first fresh leaves of spring, the warmth of it mirrored in her eyes. Light in color, like spring. Bright, clear and warm. And she smiled, not as an apology at the ends of her words, but because she was sweet, pure.

I blinked. Looked at her again and saw her dark hair stuffed under a wool cap. A few strands danced down around her rosy cheeks, and the subtle bones underneath.

"Your car? It doesn't work?"

"It works. Just not very well." Again, not a voice but the light sibilance of birds in trees and leaves budding and the clearest stream tickling the old rocks with the joy of spring.

I couldn't take it and grabbed some loose papers and rattled them around on the counter.

"Can you fix it today?"

I wanted to run. I wanted her to run. I wanted the roof to collapse with all of the rain and snow and steel so we could die right then. I knew it could only get worse.

"Your car? Today. Where is it?" My voice sounded like a field mouse being killed by a lawn mower.

"Are you OK?"

"Me? Fine. Yes. Perfect." And then shots from a machine gun—my voice that is.

"You look pale." Her concern was real. I still remember its tone. Real. Hearty even.

"It's the weather." I actually sounded normal. I'm not a big guy, so I wasn't resonant, but, still, full. A full voice. That's what I had.

"This weather really slows things up. You're right."

Now, that phrase: "You're right." It can mean a lot of different things. It can mean: "You're wrong, I'm just agreeing with you—for whatever reason." It can mean: "Go straight to hell, you asshole." It can also mean: "Leave me alone. I don't want to talk to you anymore." It has often meant: "I agree with you." But, that one is rare. This time, I think it was just a punctuation mark. As her thoughts moved on to other things, she said: "You're right," to finish that last thought. I hoped that her thoughts were moving on to me. Now that that piece of business was complete, her mind was open. I hoped.

"Where's your car, ma'am?"

"Ma'am? How old do you think I look?"

I knew she wasn't upset. Her eyes smiled. She was playing with me.

"Um. I don't know. Twenty-three?"

I knew she didn't want an answer, but I was trapped. This is when my heart took off like a rabid, wild animal.

"Twenty-three?" She looked right at me. "I am twenty-three. Good guess." Then she smiled.

I told myself to remain standing. No. Matter. What. I locked my knees. If the roof falls down, remain standing. I smiled back, but there was probably pain in it.

She had won. I would drag her out of the Sahara with my teeth at that point. I was hers.

"Twenty-three. I'm twenty-five."

"Oh, twenty-five." Her eyes drifted for the first time.

I should have lied. I'm too old. I'm too old. I know it.

But, maybe not. Maybe she hates the number twenty-five. Maybe she hates math. Maybe, when she was seven, something really bad happened to her. Oh shit! Maybe her dog died when she was seven. Her favorite dog!

"Twenty-five's a good age. A quarter of a century." Her eyes returned. Her voice. Oh, her voice returned too. She was just thinking about it. My being twenty-five. She was thinking about me. My knees tried to give, but I wouldn't let them. I must have sneered at trying to slow my heart's racing.

"I never thought of myself as a quarter of a century." My voice was full. Still. I couldn't believe it.

"Right. How about my car? I'd really like to get it looked at." She put one hand on the counter.

"Your car. Right. What's it doing?"

"It's runs, but it stalls a lot. It's really hard to start and it goes really slow. It has no pick up."

"Must be the plugs or the fuel system. Maybe an injector." I looked at her hand and then back up to her eyes really fast.

"I think it's the fuel system. I changed the plugs last weekend. So, they're new. But, I bought it used and I haven't done anything with the fuel filter and am a novice when it comes to fuel injectors," she said.

I looked at her with respect.

"How long ago did you buy it?"

"Oh, I bought it last year. From a friend. He didn't have the repair records though."

Now, I'm not opposed to boys and girls being friends. But, for some reason, when she said "he", my eyes flashed red. I don't consider myself a jealous person, but the thought of her with another guy really got me.

"Oh." I took a deep breath and forced my nervousness away. I made my heart slow until it became a dull thud. I was able to concentrate.

"OK, I'll bring up the door and you can drive it in. Will it make it in?" I was all business now, my face solid.

"I think so. It may take a minute." Her voice was distant. Her brown eyes still glowed though.

"Fine. I'll raise the door."

"OK. Thanks . . . sir." Now her eyes twinkled and I stopped. She caught me. I smiled without trying. She smiled back.

"Got me," I said. She just kept smiling. Then she turned. Not slowly, but not quickly either. She turned really well though. She was in control. It showed.

As she walked away and I unconsciously pushed the button to raise the bay door, I noticed her size for the first time. She was petite—small, but well proportioned. I thought she was huge until I saw her walk away in her long, grey skirt and brown corduroy jacket. She moved so freely. Her body flowed. It didn't saunter like some women's do; it flowed. She flowed. Like that spring air in her voice—or that clear water over rocks. She was a natural phenomenon.

"There's some butter for my biscuit." A voice behind me. Lightening. Crashes. Screams of mayhem and violence.

I turned to see Al coming toward me, his eyes on HER! I must have snarled at him.

"What's that, Al?"

"Not every day you see something like that."

"Some. Thing?"

"That's right. That thing sure ain't no T-Bird. She's a sweet little Fiat. Or a Triumph." He smiled and nodded to himself and had no idea how close to real and painful death he was. But, Al was like that. A taker.

He always had this annoying way of relating everything in the world to cars. "That sneeze sounded like the ass-end of a rusty Mustang." Or, "the rain's banging harder than a Vega with no shocks." Things like that.

Sometimes Al could get carried away with his metaphors. Like right now. Calling the most beautiful woman—no, this sublime creature—a Fiat—a thing! I saw my hands on his throat, his eyes bulging and his fat, stupid tongue turning purple.

He was way off this time. Way off.

"I can handle it Al. Fuel system." I tired to be cool. Al did weigh three hundred pounds.

"She needs her system cleaned, huh? Well, bring her on in the bay. We'll get her purring like a mint Camaro."

"Hell you will," I said under my breath. Luckily she and her sputtering car appeared in front of the open bay in the rain and snow, or maybe Al's got no attention span, because he dropped it.

"Right, Tom, what you got for me this afternoon?" He looked at me as she pulled in, his face different now, more open. It was weird, but I felt better.

"You're all full up, Al—got three in the bays already." I motioned with my arm down the garage. His eyes followed.

"Right." That's right. Sometimes I got a head like a rusty fuel tank. Won't hold nuthin'!" He laughed, slapped me on the back and disappeared into the shop. People—all people—will forever be mysteries to me.

The choking car inched into the bay beside me and she shut it down. My eyes darted to the driver. There she was, embarrassed, smiling, her cap on her head.

I wondered if she smoked as I came down the two steps into the bay. She looks too fresh. Too clean to do something so horrible to herself. I hoped she didn't. The exhaust hissed and threw up steam as I came around the hood wiping the wet snow with my curved palm.

She popped out of the driver's door to meet me.

"See? It's bad." She was still grinning, embarrassed. My heart warmed in the cold air rushing in the huge garage door. I was melting with the patchy of snow on the hood.
"Yep. Sounds bad. But, not irreparable. Why don't you pop the hood? We'll take a look."

I came around to her open door as she bent inside and searched for the lever for the hood. We brushed elbows.
"Ooops. Sorry." She clenched her teeth in a grin and dipped her chin. I couldn't say anything. That move was too perfect. But, I was able to smile back as my eyes quickly scanned

the inside of her car for cigarettes. But, I couldn't see. Her brown corduroy back blocked my view.

The hood popped and I moved back around to the front of her car. I reached under and found the catch (that's always so hard to find) and released the hood.

The warmth of the engine wafted up to me and I sniffed for gas, but smelled none.

"Well, let's take a look, ma'am." My eyes darted to hers and I saw her recognize the joke, then reject it. She said nothing, but did smile—to be polite, I'm sure—and looked down at the engine.

"Could be the hoses. I've been remiss with my hoses." She came around to the front, beside me. "Ooh, it's warm." Alive. Vivacious. These are words for her. She was excited about the warmth of the engine and emitted pure energy from her small body. And it all came out of her beautiful face and elbows, and legs—everywhere.

She reached in and yanked on a hose—testing it. Satisfied, she went to the next one. I watched her hand—uncautious, unafraid—grab the hoses firmly—test their merit.

"Where could it be leaking?" She didn't look up. She was further inspecting the engine. "I know a little about fixing things, but I can't figure this one."

I came from my daze. "Could be the fuel filter or the injectors could be clogged. I don't smell gas, so maybe it's not a leak." She straightened up and looked me dead in the face. Her eyes were right at me.

"Sounds like I brought it to the right place." Now she smiled and was kind of brighter in front of me. I quickly replayed what I said and couldn't believe it. I sounded good. I had explained something very clearly.

"I think I should leave it. I need to get back to work. I'm on my lunch break."

"OK." I absently lowered the hood, disappointed. I actually almost got to touch the inside of a car at my job. See, if she had stayed right there with me, I could have worked around on it a little bit. But, since she was going to leave it, I'd have to turn it over to one of the mechanics. That's how the shop worked. Commission. And I was the customer service guy.

"Do you need a ride back to work? We have a courtesy car." I was holding the hood with the fingers of my left hand and enjoyed the weight of it there.

"No, I'll take the bus. It's no trouble."

"Please, let me get the courtesy car for you." The thought of her on a bus did not sit well with me.

"And, if you need a car tonight, I'll get you a rental. If we can't fix yours in time."

She pursed her lips, looked at her car, then back at me. "Well, all right." Her eyes dropped. Not pouty eyes were they, but enigmatic eyes. I didn't know if she was unhappy about the courtesy car or what. I looked at her wool cap, lifted the hood until just high enough and let it bang closed.

"Let me get some info from you and I'll call for the courtesy car. I'm sure we'll get you fixed up."

I opened the door to the office for her and she passed

close by as she went up the steps and in. I came in behind her and noticed she was more animated now—in a hurry. She stopped at the counter and looked at me as I came up. Her eyes were distant now—her mind was on other things. I was uncomfortable and grabbed a form and a pen.

"OK. What's your name?" I looked at her. She was facing me, but not looking at me.

"Allison Edwards."

As I wrote it I knew I would write it again. Hopefully a lot. I asked for her work number and she gave it to me. I hoped I'd get to use that too. Maybe sometime for something other than work.

"OK, Miss Edwards. It is Miss Edwards, isn't it?"

She had on gloves now.

"Yes," she smiled, again. She knew what I was up to.

"Great."

I smiled, picked up the phone and called for the courtesy car. "It'll be just a minute. You'll be at this number until five?"

"Oh, you're not driving me?" My breath stopped. Oh. My. God.

"Um, no. I have to stay here. At the desk."

"Pity," she said, her eyes not moving from me. This woman was fearless I say! I couldn't believe it.

"I'm just a phone call away. But, I will definitely call you with an update before the end of the day."

She smiled again and seemed less busy in herself. She clasped her gloved hands in front of her coat and held me there a moment longer. I felt completely open and bullet-proof at the same time. Did she know? Could she tell?

Then the courtesy car pulled up behind her. I wanted to talk and talk and talk to her and not let her leave, but Mark, in the car, honked. She turned—flowed—around, then turned her head back. "OK, then. Thank you, Tom."

Lightening shot through my guts. How did she know my name? She answered by winking and pointing at my name tag on my chest. I stupidly looked down at it and then back at her. She was at the door—a damsel—the toe of her boot touching the floor behind her other leg, smiling again—the light of spring in here with me and the wet snow falling behind her, outside.

"It was my pleasure." I was stunned at the words as I heard them come out of my mouth.

She pushed the door. The cold rushed in. She stepped out. And was gone.

Part Two: Eggs Breaking, Colors

Upon arriving home that day from work I noticed something I had never noticed before: my apartment is, was, and forever will be, a wreck, a trash heap, a pile of papers and dust balls.

I live alone.

When you live alone and you're messy it's OK, because it's your mess. Your mess signifies your stuff, your lifestyle. And, unfortunately, I realized that evening that my lifestyle was a heap. A mess.

People say your house and how you keep it says everything about your self-image. I don't believe them though. I like my mess. It's me. And I never have anyone over that I want to impress anyway. But now, this evening, I'm having second thoughts about impressions and how to make them.

It's not that I have a lot of furniture either. I have very little. A couch. A bed. A table that is broken—of course. It's chocked up with my bible from college religion class. I sold most of my books back to the bookstore in college, but I didn't sell the bible. Not that I'm particularly religious or anything. I just thought I might read it one day.

My apartment is small. Four rooms. The couch is in its own room with the bible table. My bed's in its own room surrounded by a bunch of books. I like to read.

Then there's the kitchen. It's functional. That's all I want to say about the kitchen. The bathroom is small, but tidy in its own way. And I have a porch on the back. It's a room. Of course I can only use it when it's warm. I've been thinking about buying a chair and a blanket. Then I could read out there year 'round. I haven't really gotten around to it though.

I looked at my couch. It's low to the floor, but deep. I sleep on it sometimes. It's not that big, but neither am I. I don't take up much space.

That couch is old. Really old. But works. It's brown. Like her corduroy jacket. Brown.

I've never been a fan of brown. What is brown anyway? It's mud. The color of mud. Who wants to wear something the color of wet dirt? I don't. But, sitting or sleeping on something brown is very different from wearing something brown. It's cozy, like the earth. It's soft but solid. Also like the earth. It's supple, but just in the right places. Earth.

Looking at it I realize I don't really hate brown. I like brown hair. Long brown hair is like the Earth. It's comforting.

She has brown hair. Allison Edwards. I think she has a lot of it too. It was all up under her cap so I don't know for sure. I wonder if I'll ever see her again. We didn't get her car fixed in time. It was the fuel system. The injectors were clogged and the front fuel filter was shot along with the seal on it. We didn't have the seal. Al said we did, but we didn't. We had all of the other stuff and got it straight pretty quickly. But, we have to wait to get the seal tomorrow. Early. She said she didn't want the rental. I did talk to her on the phone. Only her voice and the memory of her. I was more confident on the phone since I couldn't see her. She sounded like sugar. Like the taste of brown sugar. That's what she sounded like.

"That's OK. I should have brought it in sooner," she said.

"I'll have the courtesy car bring you here and then we'll get you a rental until tomorrow. I'm really sorry about this," I said.

"No. It's no trouble. I don't think I want the rental though. Too much to worry about."

"Are you sure? You need transportation," I said.

"I'll take the bus," she said.

Now, who would take the bus when they could have a car? I wouldn't. What could happen to a beautiful, pure young woman on the bus? Everything. Everything bad. Have you seen who rides the bus? Bad people. I couldn't believe that she wanted to take the bus.

"You want to take the bus?"

"Oh, I don't mind."

How strong is a flower? The wind? Really strong and really beautiful, just like her, like her voice.

"If you think this is the best way," I said.

"It'll be fun. I've never ridden the bus. It's a new experience."

"You like new experiences?"

"Sure. Of course," she said.

My head began to spin. Slowly at first. But my balance was going. I had to sit.

"OK, so you'll call me tomorrow, when it's done?"

"Yes. I'll call you tomorrow." The chair squealed as I sagged into it. I would talk to her tomorrow.

"Fine Miss Edwards. We'll have you fixed up. Sorry, again, about this problem." I had to smoke.

"It's not a problem and please call me Allison."

Allison. She wants me to call her Allison. This is getting good—good!

"OK Allison. Tomorrow then."

"Thanks, Tom. Bye," she said. And she hung up. With her perfect hand, she hung up. I wondered if she had on her hat over her thick brown hair.

Hair of the Earth. Voice of the wind carrying the songs of the birds. Allison. Edwards.

I dropped onto my couch and wished I had two things. One was a broom. The other was a TV. I've never owned a TV. I think I had a broom once.

I wonder if she'll ever see this place. This heap. My heap.
Sure, she will. And I'll make her dinner. A good dinner. Healthy
with a lot of vegetables. And wine. And Perrier. I heard once
Perrier is good with a meal. Yeah, a candle light dinner in my
place. It'll be my place by then. Not my heap. I'll buy a broom.
I'm going to buy a broom right now. And a dust pan.

That's another thing. I meditate. I have to. Helps keep me
sane. Sane.

I'll have to meditate when I get back from buying a broom.

My car is a heap too. It's a heap that runs perfectly though.
I should clean it out. I don't eat a lot of junk food, but it looks
like it, in my car. Who the hell rides in my car but me though?
No one. So, it doesn't matter that the back's full of bags with
grease spots and empty french fry containers. The front's full of
stuff too. Cigarette boxes, empty soda bottles. Stuff. Mess.

I don't care though. It runs perfectly. I've got all the
systems in complete check. I change the oil regularly and keep
everything up. I love to work on it and do all of the time.

It's American, which is OK. Easy to get cheap parts. I'm
thinking to paint it. The paint on it is good, but it's green. I
don't like green on cars. Green is for the trees or eyes or frogs,
not for cars. I guess I could have not bought it. But, I did and
I guess the green's not so bad when I think that I didn't pay that
much for it. I mean, I did get a good deal. So, that's something
and that something makes the green a little less, I don't know,
problematic.

It started instantly, of course. And once the transmission

warmed up it ran well.

I missed all of the red lights on the way to the store. I hate stop and go. That's not driving.

At the store I parked really close. A good parking spot is a good omen in these times. America. If any Indian Shamans or Medicine Men were around, driving cars, they would feel the good vibrations associated with a good parking spot. And they would look up to the sky, as I did, and thank with deep reverence as I did.

Now, I'm not a big fan of pre-fab, puked-up buildings. Have you ever seen the nation's capitol? It's big. It's made out of stone and it's beautiful. It's a living monument. It took years to build.

This place I was walking into under the spitting rain/snow was the reverse of our nation's capitol. It was brick, which is almost stone. It was rectangular and it had a flat roof. Practical, I guess. But. What's practical about ugly? What's practical about something that looks like a box with sliding doors? Where I work looks exactly the same as this place. Did you ever read The Fountainhead? I know there were once architects that cared about form and not just function. I know there were passionate men with really good minds once. They made stuff that was practical because it was beautiful. Functional because its form was inspirational. And still is. Go to our nation's capitol sometime. You'll see what I mean.

But I ignored the damn, ugly uninspiring box I was walking into. I was on a mission of change. With a broom I would transform my heap of an apartment into a clean heap of an apartment. And the change wasn't just for me. It wasn't really for me at all.

These places are so bright and they have that musak going all the time. Is this supposed to make me happy? To make me a happy shopper? If it was, it didn't. But, I didn't care. I was moving fast.

I found the brooms pretty quickly. The cheapest one was fifteen dollars. Fifteen dollars. For a broom. I had a choice. Change would happen if I laid down the cash. If I didn't lay down the cash things would remain the same. Money equals change. That's America. I guess.

I wouldn't have felt so sick if they had had a wooden broom for fifteen dollars. But, I had to buy a yellow plastic broom with my fifteen dollars.

I felt it in my hands. It was light. It felt cheap and glared like a big fake pencil in those lights. Was I supposed to be happy about sweeping with my yellow broom? Bright and sterile as it was. I'm rarely happy about things bright or sterile.

I paid cash. Sixteen thirty-two for a big, sterile, yellow broom to bring about change in my life. I wished it were wood. Just wood that would wear while my hands worked. Wood that would get smooth with use. Wood that could be used as kindling if I needed it. Wood. But my tool of change was plastic. Impersonal and meant to be that way.

Wood would show my change. As it wore down and

smoothed with age, I could look at it and remember working with it. Not this big, ugly fake pencil though. It would always look the same: sterile, dull, ugly. I guess the bristles will wear, but, still.

I ran to my car in the wet flakes. It was now snowing more than raining. I guess it had gotten colder.

Just as my door shut, I realized I didn't get a dust pan.

I'll use a magazine, I guess.

Part Three: Index Markets

1. Death is very unsettling to me. Not my own death, but other people's deaths.

2. Two types of people—those who tell others what to think and those who want to be told what to think.

3. Meat grinder body—the effective way to dispose of a body.

4. "You're like a magazine. Everything's on the cover. Obvious."

"Are you saying I'm for sale? That I'm some cheap rag?"

"No."

"Yes you are. I can't believe you. What . . . who the hell do you think you are? Jesus Christ. What an asshole!"

I was sure she would leave. But she didn't. Did she really agree with me, even though she missed my point? Her furrowed brow and down-cast eyes told me something else—something other. She has low self-esteem. Or she likes abuse. Something is not right.

"I wasn't saying that, Allison. I wasn't saying you're cheap."

She glanced up, her fire dimming.

"You're not that. What I'm saying was, is, that I know you well. I can tell how you feel, sometimes. You've been so honest with me that I know you well and some things are obvious about you to me—like the cover of a magazine."

It all came out wrong. How could anyone say such shit to someone they genuinely admired—someone they genuinely liked?

"Tom, you're a smart guy. But sometimes you say really stupid things."

"I know." All too well.

"Look, I didn't mean to be mean."

"Stop. Words make it worse. Can we go?"

I looked down at my half-drunk coffee, flashed back up to her and smiled weakly. I raised my eyebrows to try to help lighten the air.

"Sure. Yeah. Let's go."

She stood up quickly, pulled on her favorite wool cap and walked out the door.

I cleared the dishes into a nearby bus tray and followed her out.

Her back was to me. The air was crisp and refreshing. I knew she wasn't mad. Probably because she didn't care enough to be so. But I didn't let that bother me.

"Would you still like to go to the movie," I asked.

She didn't turn, her face solid. I noticed, maybe for the first time, how good her posture was, how straight her shoulders were.

"Sure. I'd like to go to the movie," she said.

I was a little surprised. She noticed, peripherally.

"Do you not want to go?" She turned only her head. I couldn't see her neck. It was a weird movement. Robotic.

"Oh yeah, I want to go. Definitely."

She reached out her bare hand. I could only see her fingers. Her coat was big, frumpy almost. I wasn't scared. I was confused. Why is she being nice? Why to me now? Did she want to be in charge, in control?

"Well?" She could be so charming when she was insistent. One of the things I really loved. She could be so subtly motivating. She didn't make me do anything. At least things I didn't already really want to do.

I took a couple of her small fingers in my right hand. I still remember their warmth. And we turned up the street to go to the movie.

Walking on the cold concrete of that winter day I know I was truly happy. I didn't need to look at her, nor she at me. Only our hands talked—and lightly so. So sibilant, insouciant was our manual communication on that cold day. So perfect. I think she felt it too. That made me even more happy. The knowing.

The air was clear even though the sky was overcast. I love the heaviness of a grey sky. It's comforting. The world is smaller, not as overwhelming. Things are quieter too. I only heard our footsteps. The cars didn't even exist. The people didn't exist. None of that typical urban noise was present. Only sounds of four feet. Only the light conversation of our hands. And the air. The crisp life-giving air.

She wore clogs often, as she did today. Their heavy sounds still echo in my head—not with violence though. I'm not angry at the memory of them. Not angry at all. But not joyous either.

They were such a contrast to my rubber souls. I could feel the sounds her feet made. My own feet were squishy-silent. Maybe we walked in step together. I think we did. And her clogs clomped on the cold concrete and I moved in tandem with them, connected so sweetly by a few fingers, to her. Connected so richly, so deeply, to her. Nothing else mattered. It rarely did when I was with her.

Part Four: Willow, Winnow, Wound

I think she let the aggression of earlier go—away in the breeze maybe—and so I did too. It was better this way. No talking, but communicating. Out here in the world. In ourselves, but out of them too. Here together. This way.

We neared the marquee and it was bright. A bastion in that grey day. A new experience not calling to me, but waiting. Ready. And there I was. Little me with this angel. This dark angel of unique light, holding my hand. I felt her fingers lace into mine. Their supple strength not forceful, not overwhelming, but perfect. Her fingers fit so well in mine. I'm glad I had forgotten to put on my gloves. I'm glad she had too. Maybe she forgot on purpose. For me.

We were under the marquee. She released me gently and let me buy the tickets. I couldn't see her for those few moments, but I was glad. Because I knew she was there. I knew it. And she was waiting for me.

And the air. And the clouds. And the silence. And, then, her face. Nestled under that wonderful cap, surrounded by strands of that magnificent hair. And her big, brown coat which I didn't like, but I did. Charming all the way to her knees. And her tights. Black. Thick. I knew she had on a short wool skirt. I knew. And her clogs. Her shoes around her feet. She didn't think about her shoes. She didn't hear them. I know she didn't care. She was distracted. Her cheek turned to me. Just a hint of rose over the strong jaw. Then she turned. And her eyes. Set back under her light brow, not heavily, but just so, solidly, down in there. Enticingly. They were jewels. Deepest brown. With a hint of yellow. The light in the dark. So enticing. So rewarding. Some may say she had an intense glare. Impatient almost. But I knew better. I knew what made those eyes so brilliant and so richly dark and deep at the same time. Her soul. The soul of an angel. But an angel on Earth. In life. Living, breathing, heaving mountainous life through those eyes, those dark jewels.

Sometimes in the mirror I see those eyes, her eyes. Especially when I'm not looking. And they look back at me with that same intensity, that same assurity and I'm not afraid. There is no fear in those eyes in the mirror and no reason to be afraid. They say how unreasonable fear truly is. How irrational, illogical, unimportant.

And then they're gone—those eyes—and all I see is my own blank visage in the mirror. Clouded by trepidation and fear, growing, growling fear. With no medicine, no salve for my own dim reflection, I am not resplendent. I am not alive. I am not whole. Those eyes—her eyes—the centerpiece of God's own wish for true life. They fade in the mirror and all I see is me. Myself. And it's too real. No hope. Not the hope of that one, my sweet angel, my dark angel, my life.

"Tom?"

I blinked and shuttered at the same time. The silent grey world returned and I felt peace. So slight, but so real. And the eyes spoke.

"Hello? Anybody home?" she asked.

I fumbled. My mouth wouldn't work.

"Shall we go in?" she said.

"Yes," weakly, I finally said.

"Are you OK?" she whispered.

I think she must have known right then and there. Her rhetoric was obvious to me and she knew I knew she knew.

"It's a beautiful day." I stepped closer to her.

"Yes. It's quiet. I like quiet sometimes." She hooked my elbow and led me to the doors.

"Me too."

And we went in. We went in.

Part Five: My Only Friend

After it fell apart I wasn't overly concerned. I wasn't worried. The world didn't end. The sun continued to rise. The air still gave life.

—

I have these internal moments where the world—everything, everyone—is a pictureshow out there and if I catch myself being drawn too close to the screen I move back, back to the back row. A slow fade.

But, the show does go on, doesn't it?

—

There wasn't even a hole in my life or anything like that. I did care though. I cared and I worried. I worried about her. I worried about her eyes and what would happen to them, what they would see. Angels can be so damn fickle.

There was nothing immediate about the dismissal. Actually it was rather slow. Like a building with its mortar slowly unhardening—turning back into mud. First the walls of sturdy bricks sag. Slowly. But quickly they gain some momentum, some energy. Gravity pulls the building sliding down into a pile of rubble. A heap of mud. Not drips. A viscous slipping. Sliding down. Back to Earth. That's what it was like. But, you know, we didn't build the building in the first place, she and I. It was like we moved in. We were tenants. Only a monthly rent.

And the building turned to mud. The mortar slipped under our feet. It wasn't like an Earthquake, something sudden. No, not like that. It was a lugubrious sliding. A slipping. Maybe it started as soon as we moved in. Maybe the vertigo of the solid turning to mush happened immediately and what I thought was euphoria was not jubilant. Maybe it was a sinking euphoria. The building sinking under us, under our weight. Maybe a chunk of it fell off and down and down, bang on the ground. Maybe there were some chunks that fell off. But, mostly, it was this sliding. This heavy sliding.

But, she wasn't heavy. She was light. Wings in her eyes. Wings to fly her away from the sinking. Wings to keep her hovering just above the sinking floor. The sinking building.

Maybe I was heavy. Maybe not. I really don't think so. Maybe I was a chunk that fell.

—

I'm sitting on my couch listening to this experimental music by this sound artist Griffin. This music on this album, Pointed, was made with pots and pans, a few instruments and effects and a 4-track cassette recorder. Home-made. But, the sounds. The sounds, and the environments they created were completely enveloping me—and infusing me. There's so much life there and I could feel myself moving, moving with the sounds—the music so unlike anything I'd ever heard—or experienced—direct emotion in sound—and moving—the energy of creation in sound—finding its own shape—riding through tunnels and soaring in space and crashing with waves. Rising up and then pulling low. Expanding as it moves—me with it—it with me—all of me. Gathering me into its momentum.

And then she came in—right in my door—the metallic sounds of sprinklers or sparklers or little digital bits slamming into each other and flying, gathering, and flying—around us—filling the space—down into the cracks you can't even see.

I stood up—that force of moving sound around us—and then slowly, slowly, faded the volume down, and down, down to silence.

And she said nothing, with her voice at least. Standing there. Just apart from me. Breathing. Her energy now filling the room—not as the music had—but with her own, flowing signature.

And I focused on that. Her energy. Her.

It was her manner that spoke so clearly. Above her few words. My apartment was clean. The broom-pencil in the closet.

"How was your day?"

I am there. Not with anticipation, not with joy, but my eyes were fixed on her there.

Out there.

—

"It was good. Long. No longer than others. It just seemed long."

She stopped, further sensing the not-usual feeling in the room. There was something other than ordinariness to interact with now. We could yank down to the mundane, but neither of us wanted to. We wanted to gather. And ride.

Her shoulders relaxed down and she dropped off her coat to reveal herself—well, the next layer at least. Her sweater was an interplay of color and non-color. Light and dark concealing the real shape beneath, the fixture of her femininity.

—

She came over to me not to kiss, but to embrace.

—

I held her, warmed her. I formed to her, my arms delicately around her back.

—

She breathed out deeply. Her warm breath catching her

vocal chords and making a chesty sound. A sound of warmth, comfort. At this point I could believe it. I knew she meant it. In her deep, chesty sound she was confiding in me so much. Telling me of her woe and thanking me for my comfort at the same time. Happily. Warm—together—filling each other's needs. A moment of serene wholeness. Delicious. Like a perfect mug of hot chocolate.

There's that brown again.

It was what she needed. With her laced fingers in the small of my back, she looked right into my eyes. I knew. Instantly, I knew. She was ready. Willing. Wanting. Her eyes.

Our kisses were not sweet, sick puppy-dog licking. Nor were they from any innocence or concern. Never was there a concern with getting it right. Our mouths just fit. Our tongues moved, gracefully, slowly with a rhythm beyond conscious control. A rhythm prescribed by God. He was in our kisses, our adulations of oral bliss. The feeling of her mouth against mine—our movements together—was a feeling not just rare, but impossible to mimic, impossible to recreate with something or someone else. Like the sensation of a cigarette. There is nothing like it—nothing its equal. These were our kisses. No time. No thought. No human boundary. Our souls melding.

Again she looked up at me. Her eyes telling me more than yes. Telling me fully "of course." And, quietly in the back, "Thank you." My own eyes mirrors. Not distilled mockery nor feigned joy. More. Deeper. Realer.

She released me. I followed. She turned. I stopped.

"Tom. I feel better. Warm."
"Me too."

"I do want to go to your room with you now."

———

I turned and looked out the door—toward the room.
"But, there's something else."
I looked back at her and remained firm.
"Please don't take this the wrong way."

———

"How could I?" I blurted out, not defensively though.

———

"I want our sex, our love-making to be a result. And well,
I'm not ready yet."
I was relieved. Pleased even.
"Is that all?"
"Yes," she blurted this time. She was trying to make a point.
Trying to make me understand. And I did although I don't think
she knew I did.

———

"A result." Her eyes dropped. Her face turned away.

"Of course. I feel the same way. I'm not worried. It'll

come."

I knew she wanted me to talk.

—

"I'm not ready either. I'm happy, very happy, that we can just be."

She looked up. She was happy. Her eyes were light again. I understood. But, somewhere in the back of her there was something else. Like a valve clicked off and stopped the flow.

"And when the time is right," I came to her, lightly touched her hand, her fingers, my eyes on hers, "we'll know. We'll know together and we won't have to speak. At least with our voices we won't speak."

I was setting the stage. My mouth ran on. She was pleased, I think. I was pleased with my calm words—my subtle resolve.

"So, let's not talk. Let's . . . something. Let's do some thing."

"Yeah. I feel like I want to DO something."

She inspired it, I know. My idea was not mine. It came from her. From her being.

"Let's go down to the river. It's crystal cold. And we will dangle our feet in the water. I'm sure it's icy, impossibly freezing. And we'll sit there until we can't take it and then we'll sit there five minutes longer. We'll keep time. We'll make ourselves wait, with our feet freezing for . . . Five. More. Minutes."

"Yes!" She jumped on me in a tight hug.

"Yes." I was so pleased that she was pleased.

!

Quickly she threw her coat back on. I grabbed mine and we rushed out of the door. We were both hopeful, excited.

!

Outside, the night was black. No stars. And the air stung our noses with its reckless wisps.

!

She smiled up to me, her dark hair a cape behind her. A thick cape of energy in the wind. Solid energy. Not erratic.

!

My car roared alive under us, the blackness only daunted by my dashboard light.

I looked to her and saw an empty paper coffee cup pinched between her fingers.

"Looks like you're slipping after your sipping."

I knew she was joking. Her full lips in an elastic grin.

!

"Right. From this morning. But only one cup. Not bad for a really messy guy like me."

"Right." She dropped it over her shoulder, over the seat to the back.

We both tingled with electricity as I floored the car away into the night.

!

In the intermittent streetlights I noticed her hair shining like black silk. Not crumply velvet, but smooth, sleek black silk— the shine deep from its layers.

She hummed lightly with the music from the radio. She knew I watched. She knew I lovingly watched her with deep admiration. We both were so alive. So poised. So vibrant. And her hands tapping her lap. Tapping her heavy coat over her lithe legs. Her hair. The sweetly sharp outline of her jaw, her pertinent nose, her thick lips. Lit in the vertigo of the flashing, passing lights. She knew I watched her—observed her, regarded her beautiful.

And then we were at the river. The slight fear that she felt shot into me and was absorbed by my warmth from her. My guts felt her fear, her trepidation. She knew I could take it. She could rely on it and that made her warm, which made me warm.

At the edge the deep water moved heavily, silently. Its push indomitable. Commanding reverence in its silent movement. Rich with deep life—the heavy essence of life.

We stood in the silence—the lights of the city twinkling in the cold distance.

Our shoulders touched. We didn't move. We prayed. Prayed to the river and its life.

Under her hair I could see her lips pull into a grin. I knew it was time.

I dropped down and pulled off my boots. She kicked off her clogs. My guts quivered at her socked feet. So perfect. The architecture of her foot perfect in the tight sock. I so desperately wanted to see those white feet in the clear icy water. To see the arch, move back and forth—better than touching. Knowing that intimate part on display for me, for the river.

I hoped she wanted to see my feet too. I hoped she liked them.

I slipped off my socks with my index finger—she followed my movement. On the rocks in the darkness, the coldness, her feet radiated light. The feet—so important to life—their understanding so simple, so obvious—no explanation.

The air shot out from me in a short burst.

"Ready?" She giggled.

"Yes." I knew she didn't care about my feet the way I cared about hers. I didn't care.

We walked up, she grabbed my arm with mock fear. Then we hunched and squatted and finally sat together—on the edge, just above the freezing black river. She was still clutching my arm. The big rock was cold under me, through my pants.

She squeezed my arm and sucked the night air in through her nose. We looked down at the rushing dark water.

And our feet went in.

The exhilaration of orgasm comes close to that feeling. Plunging your feet into liquid ice rushes the blood through you. I fought to stay conscious. She was quiet. She took the pain and was waiting for the pleasure—the rush up in her. I stretched my feet to float just under the surface. I could feel the strong flow between my toes, tickling me, tickling my soul. Electric liquid ice propelling that rush in me too.

Her jaw muscles tightened as she stretched her toes apart, absorbing the water—the liquid ice. She was starting to enjoy it.

We trembled and shook like baby birds as the sensation deepened.

"I know how to die of frostbite now. I know the calm that comes from being extremely cold." She straightened her back.

I hummed deeply, meditatively. In my chest.

"Five. More. Minutes." I held my wrist out in front of us so we could both see my watch.

Her chin dipped and she set herself to the task. She exhaled quickly, her noise high in the register. I harmonized her with my deep, chesty hum. We sounded together, feeling the ice, the exhilaration, the cold, the possibility of death.

Her hand slowly tightened around my wrist. My erection began. "Don't think. Feel. Feel." She didn't look at me but closed her eyes and continued to hum.

My erection grew, throbbing, pulsing with thick hot blood untouched, but pushed, by that ice water and of our mingled sounds as my feet were frozen stone licked by ancient, freezing, freezing moonlight.

Time evaporated and she locked her eyes, the eyes of God, on me. Her grip tightened. Her jaw solid. Her song going high. We stared, we glared. We were together. We were locked immobile.

Then her song growled low. Raspy and sweet her voice caressed me—growing stronger. My feet were gone. I quickly glanced at hers. Immobile. Perfect in the clear, dark water. Ten little toes, perfectly sculpted to the arch and the heal—God their craftsman.

Quickly again back to her. She was panting. Heavy like a panther—a big cat—her lids half-low and falling with the hot air from her throat. The hot air from her throat.

The five minutes became seven. We stared again at each other, my cock twitching, tingling. Her lip quivering. Frozen to each other—no pain, only ecstasy. Pure electric ecstasy.

Her fingernails dug into my wrist, puncturing me. Stopped. Slowed. Silence. Only feeling. No feet. Silence.

Then the quick, pulsing rush of it all.

And I exploded. A long stream of liquid energy and lightening running out of me with fire of a million suns— white hot fire—looooooooong through that tiny little hole in my manhood—shot from me.

"Hup!   Fug!   Shotz!"   White ice freezing light. "BUUUUUUUUUAGH!!"

And I fell back, moaning, she with me, I still in her grip and I screamed and hoarsely foundered, my back arched, my heart racing, racing, racing. The front of my pants was soaked. Her nails in my skin. GOD! Nirvana. The pure rush obliterated me—blew me apart at the atoms—I was nothing and everything at once.

Her low moans swam around me—warm movement—long and low—out of her and into the cold, crisp air as I realized she had exploded too. But inside. Controlledly on her inside with her feet in the moonlit freezing ice water river. All holding her inside. The only sign of this her hot steam breath rushing away alive in the moonlight, away in the crisp air, over that deep, dark, freezing water.

And I was flaccid, rubber. Still she held me.

Breathing. And slowly. Breathing. Great exhausted clouds of mist in the night—my breath. Her breath. Mingling. Above us. Frozen. Then away.

I rolled onto my shoulder and continued on top of her. She wrapped her arms around me. She squeezed me with all of her strength. My arms were dead. I couldn't respond.

She licked the side of my face—her rough, edgy tongue up me—warm, wet, then a slick of chill in the cold.

Weakly, I raised my head, my eyes, to see her. And they were there. Dark jewels in the night. Wide. Bringing all of the light in. Her gaping mouth exhaling. Slowly. Now. Heat. Warmth in the mist on my face. My feeling. She felt my dead weight on her and she grinned and then laughed. Cackled really. Her chest jumping under me.

There was nothing else. And her emptiness was as hollow as the sky—the great black dome of night and I knew she was done with me. Maybe she didn't know yet. But I did. I could see it there—the nothing that waited. And it just wasn't her fault. This was true too. Deep currents like the black river there do move and we just never, ever understand them.

Not that she was a monster. No. I don't need to create the idea of an opposite to make a point. No, she was much more integrated than that. And without her, something would just not be there—not any dramatic closing finish, but an absence. Gone.

I rolled off. She sat up and, in so doing, brought her feet out of the water. I followed her motion—sat up and pulled my feet out too. They were numb. White. Ice. Cold. Stone. Numb. I looked at her feet. The same. Too white.

She instinctively brought them closer to her, bending her knees, cupping them in her hands. I did the same. I rubbed and rubbed—slid my fingers into the cracks and moved them back and forth. Squeezed my toes. Then she turned on her bottom toward me and put her feet in my direction. I knew the idea and followed.

We put the soles of our feet together there by the river in the night and we rubbed. We rubbed up and down and back and forth. But we said nothing—always our eyes locked. All the sweetness of her was still there. All of the things I had ever thought, seen and felt were still true. I think, maybe, she knew this too.

And soon there was tingling—pins poking in—little pricks of pain as feeling returned. And then warmth. A little, then spreading. And soon we knew that we could stand.

And soon we did stand and soon, now, we felt the cold air on our faces and the cold grass under our feet—on our soles—and now we clasped hands and, together, we looked down at our shoes—her clogs—my dirty boots—our socks—and now we looked at each other again—and now, we looked up the hill and started toward the car, barefoot, together—away. One foot. Another foot. Up the hill. Drawn along. Falling up. Our feet to our legs, to hips, torsos, guts, chests, to arms and heads, moving, but falling. Falling up the hill away from the river, up to the hill there and the sky beyond, above, yes, fal

white out, 1994

Outro:

So, you wanted me to write this thing. So I did.

Jeremy Witt was born in Richmond, Virginia in 1970 and holds a BA in Theater Arts and English Literature from Randolph-Macon College.

He has had numerous shows of his photography and created works in many areas of the arts. He, too, has designed and edited many projects for publication.

He lives in rural Virginia.

Visit www.jeremywittphotography.com and www.jeremywittart.com to see more of his work.